THE CO

Ardhendu Bose, a fatherless middle-class Bengali boy brought up by a domineering and vicariously ambitious mother, tries to escape from the failures of life in the arms of his Punjabi girlfriend, a BPO job that is sheer drudgery, the mindless somersaults of Crystal, his six-year-old Labrador, and in the company of the never-say-die and Texan drawl-trawling Manoj.

But everything is set to change overnight. A loser from a B-grade Indian business school, Ardhendu is summoned for an interview by RED, the fourth largest Life Sciences company in the world. His life takes a turn for the better, or so he believes, when he is chosen over an IIM hopeful, to be Executive Assistant to President, India Operations, RED. Finally, he gets a life, works with people with exotic names he pronounces effortlessly as though he were one of them, drinks their fine spirits, attends their parties, and climbs the ladder rapidly. Till that epiphanic moment in a penthouse balcony when it becomes clear that there is a price to pay to be a part of that world…of predators.

A frightful and thought-provoking tale of hunts blurring lines between humans and vampires, *The Company RED* is the first novel of the RED trilogy by Shantanu Dhar.

Shantanu Dhar earned a Bachelor's in English Literature from the University of Pune, Nashik and a Post-graduate degree in Human Resource Development from Pittsburg State University, Kansas, USA. Currently employed with a major Indian conglomerate, he writes regularly for business magazines on human behaviour at the workplace, and has been deeply inspired by Greek tragedies and Gothic novels in his fictional writing.

He lives in Greater Noida with his wife and two young children, and spends his early mornings cycling on open wide roads and his evenings listening to his eclectic collection of jazz at a decibel his family members and neighbours may have much to say about.

THE COMPANY RED

Shantanu Dhar

OM
Om Books International

First reprint 2011

Om Books International

Corporate & Editorial Office
A-12, Sector 64, Noida 201 301
Uttar Pradesh, India
Phone: +91 120 477 4100
Email: editorial@ombooks.com
Website: www.ombooksinternational.com

Sales Office
4379/4B, Prakash House, Ansari Road
Darya Ganj, New Delhi 110 002, India
Phone: +91 11 2326 3363, 2326 5303
Fax: +91 11 2327 8091
Email: sales@ombooks.com
Website: www.ombooks.com

ISBN: 978-93-80070-21-6

10 9 8 7 6 5 4 3 2

Printed in India by Thomson Press (India) Limited

To

Dr. G.C. Dey of HCL, the gentle, patient and the brilliant physician. Without your expert medical advice, this would have been just another story!

Bonti. Without your unflinching support, encouraging feedback and insistence that I keep my deadlines, this would not have happened!

Sanjiv Dange. Thanks for reappearing after 20 years and pointing the book in the right direction.

Satish Kaushik. Thank you for listening to the outline two years ago (when *The Company RED* was just a fantasy) and your perpetual encouragement since then!

The tale of the hunt, if told by the lion,
would be a totally different one.

1

It was a year and a half before the Commonwealth Games.

BIG FRIES!

Ardhendu Bose stared at the notice board unbelievingly. A burger company was coming in on Monday to his MBA institute for pre-placement talks.

"Great!" He thought to himself. "After two years of this crap, I'll get to *flip burgers* at a drive-through! Ah, the joy!"

Manoj Khewsara, his classmate of two years and best friend since school, sauntered up to him. "You mean, that's it?"

Ardhendu nodded. "Man, can I get a refund?"

He looked around at the walls of the corridor; they were being painted. Unfinished patches stood out at the corners of the walls and overlapped the edges of the ceiling haphazardly. Most painters had mastered this technique.

Manoj noticed that his best friend had missed out on his remark. He watched as Ardhendu took in the unfeeling blue of the walls.

"Yep, beautifying the bride for the placement days, just as they are trying with this city. Covering up manholes with quicksand," remarked Manoj.

Ardhendu shrugged his shoulders dejectedly. As he turned around, he saw a suited figure waddling down the corridor towards them…Ravi Merajkar, Dean of the institute. There was only one bottle of liquor in Ardhendu's home — a vintage Hennessey Bras D'or Napoleon. His mother had, of course, guarded it fiercely for what seemed like a million years. Oddly, the dean reminded Ardhendu of it. Perhaps, it was the shape…

"See? We have a Fortune 500 company coming into campus. Your future is made!"

"Er, Sir, are we getting any others?" Ardhendu asked politely, trying hard not to stare at the orange tie that dangled above the dean's wayward midriff.

"Oh, yes!" The dean affirmed looking at the two youngsters disdainfully. For a while it seemed as if he were going to mumble a spell that would make them disappear into the ground, but no, he was in a good mood today. So he preened.

"We have GE, Wipro, Axis, ICICI, and perhaps two others next week!"

Ardhendu's eyebrows shot up. "Their operations divisions?"

Suddenly, the dean seemed unnerved. Then after a brief moment, he regained his composure. This time he did not bother to hide his contempt for the two wastrels with whom he had the misfortune of interacting on this fine morning.

"No, but their BPO arms," he snapped back with an air of finality, peering at them through his 1920s steel-rimmed spectacles. The lenses had jaundiced with time.

Ardhendu sensed challenge in those small patronising eyes. An old familiar sinking feeling in his stomach oppressed him again. The sparkle in his eyes gradually dimmed. It was an effort to make sure that the rest of his face did not give anything away. So he put out a brave smile, nodding at the dean.

"So, gentlemen, iron those shirts and dust down those suits. Your future waits!" He waved his hand with a flourish over the notice board and looked disappointed as the grand gesture did not elicit a swishing sound. But life does not always imitate a Tamil action-film, and Merajkar was no Rajinikanth. So he turned about stylishly, and walked off without sparing them a second glance.

The wastrels stood silently for a couple of minutes. Ardhendu looked at the Organisational Development book in his hands. It felt heavy and lifeless. Suddenly, the last two years came rushing back to him...his lousy GMAT score, his flunking the CAT, his mother struggling to put together a hefty donation for his admission, classes that relied on rote learning, boring lectures, silly assignments... He longed for Veena. Somehow, in her arms, he could escape these realities...she always had time for him, smoothed his brow, brought back a smile on his face...

"So buddy, our future waits," Manoj interrupted his reverie. "Hi, this is Saaandiee. I'm callin from Gimme Yore Money Or Yore Life Bank. Since we caan't loot yew in broad daylight, we're offerin yew this credit card that will milk yew fer the rest of your life. So wen d'ya sign up?"

Ardhendu couldn't help laughing at Manoj's fake American accent. "So this is what you get when you enroll into a B-Grade business school," he observed philosophically.

"B-Grade, says who?" Manoj asked pretending to be shocked at what he had just heard.

"Well, Gokul Chand Institute of Management is really no Harvard."

"I agree. But it still is an IIM," Manoj said firmly.

"What do you mean?"

Manoj fixed Ardhendu with a piercing gaze. "Indian Institute of Merajkar."

Both of them burst into laughter.

⌒

Veena was waiting at home. She jumped on him as soon as he walked in.

"Wait, what are you doing…"

"It's OK. Your mom isn't home yet."

"But…"

It was the scent. Not sensuous but flowery, powdery, something that mothers wore…soothing, comforting. The rustle of the cotton kurta Veena wore was familiar, comforting. Her hair pushing against his cheek, soft, clean, comforting. Her light blue salwaar kameez, easy on the eyes, comforting…

He let go, standing there in the comfort of her embrace, shutting the world out. That was what he did when his mother comforted him…shut out the world.

The sound of his mother's footsteps was enough to make him push Veena away instinctively.

Veena flashed a sly smile at him as his mother entered the house.

Anjali Bose wore her usual light blue cotton sari, crumpled a bit from driving home all the way from Delhi University's south campus in her decrepit Matiz. Her jaws stiffened at the sight of Veena, but loosened almost immediately, as if aware that her expression might betray her feelings.

"So, what's new today?"

"Er, nothing much Mom. Preparing for a few placement interviews."

"Any big names?"

"Oh! The usual suspects. This year we have a host of BPO companies."

"Well, that's the way it is today. India is the back-office country of the world, but the way costs are spiralling, we may lose out to the Philippines..." Anjali muttered as she put everything she carried on the kitchen counter: books, groceries, some chicken for Ardhendu. She looked around the little flat, her keen eyes taking in the sofa. Nothing unruffled. Either the kids had been behaving themselves, or she had returned too soon. For a second, she felt like an intruder. Then the warmth of the beige walls enveloped her. The sofa, the settee, the TV, the DVD player, the little Sony CD player, the *kiranawala's* calendar on the wall, the little potted plants, sunlight filtering in through the windows — this was the place where she had raised this young man since he was a five year old; the only place in the world she could call home, her home. No one, not even that undeserving girlfriend of her son could make her feel like an intruder here.

Not this girl, for God's sake! Why did her son have to be so controlled by her? Why, she was even older than him by a couple of years. Why, oh why couldn't he have found someone nicer, better, non-controlling, sweet, caring, like, like *her own self*. Oh, why, why couldn't he have been assertive, strong, manly, cool, like, like...

"Look, if you have a boyfriend or something, I can make this easy for you. I'll just tell them that I don't like you."

That was the young and dashing Amitava Bose.

It was 5 pm. They were at Anjali's home at Dum Dum, Calcutta. The young Amitava, on his way to the US, to pursue a doctorate in Medicine, had been 'accompanied' by his parents to her home to meet her. After tea, with the customary 'wouldn't-you-like-to-see-our-home routine', the parents had disappeared — the Bengali, cultured way of leaving the prospective bride and groom alone.

That comment was good enough to melt the virginal Anjali completely. She knew then that this would be the only man she would ever love in her whole life. She looked deep into his eyes and said, boldly, "No, I don't. Never have had one."

Amitava smiled at her gently. She gazed at him in awe — tall, six feet, broad shouldered, biceps that sprung out of his tight black T-shirt, long black hair without sideburns, tight blue jeans over a pair of spotlessly white Nikes, dark, glowing, healthy skin that could only be the result of lifting weights regularly, his masculinity shone through, reassuring her that he would hold her, protect her and take care of her forever.

"Auntie, you must be tired. Would you like some tea?" Veena was sweetness personified.

Anjali returned reluctantly to the present. As her gaze fell on her son, her first thoughts were — five feet eight inches, round face, no biceps, signs of a small paunch beneath a dull blue T-shirt, jeans slumped on hips, held together by a belt, dirty shoes, unkempt hair, sallow skin and a permanent slouch. She wondered why his father's genes had given him a miss.

"Sure Veena, that would be lovely," Anjali said without meeting Veena's eyes. The attempt at impressing the future mother-in-law was not wasted on her. She smiled at her son as his girlfriend disappeared into the kitchen.

"I hope she will still offer me tea after the two of you get married."

"If she doesn't, I will." Ardhendu smiled at his mother and put his arms around her. Anjali returned her son's hug warmly. It was only on rare occasions now that her baby hugged her. She kissed his forehead affectionately.

"It would be good to see you settled soon." The concern in her voice did not go unnoticed.

"I will Mom, I will," said Ardhendu, breaking away from her embrace. He turned away, trying to shake off that voice in his head which had begun to churn guilt. He would now go into a shell. Communication between him and her would break down for the next few hours as it had happened several times already in the past. Only, each time this happened anew, Ardhendu took longer to come out of his emotional exile.

She turned away from him and looked fleetingly at his father's photograph on the wall. How she missed having him around. She tried to shake off that thought as she walked into the kitchen to help Veena who was struggling with the pot. Looking at the mess her son's girlfriend had made, she bit her lip. The thought of having to see this Punjabi girl inside her nice Bengali kitchen for the rest of her life made her wince.

"Beta, haven't you made tea before?" she asked sweetly.

That night as she began to drift off to sleep, she cursed herself for holding a grudge against the girl her son loved.

"What a great professor of Psychology you are, Anjali!" she chided herself.

2

Manoj was at his Texan drawl again. "No Mayam, what yew have paid was jes the innerest amount. Yew still need to payyup the principal. Yeah, I know Mayam. May I have the check number, pleeese?"

Ardhendu looked at him: square Indian face, teeth that needed braces but never had them, thin, prickly moustache, curly, unruly hair and a promising paunch…he looked anything but the cool American white dude he was trying to be on the phone.

"You done?"

Manoj grinned at him. He hung up, removed his earphones and sat them on the desk. Staring at the clocks on the wall, he got up from his seat. 7 pm in New York, and 5 am in Noida. The walls were painted violet and blue. The company's logo was just about everywhere. The workers were glued to their desks, earphones strapped to their heads, talking into their mikes with serious faces and fake accents, talking through time zones, milking hundreds of unsuspecting lower middle class Americans stretched already by unemployment, the loss of pension funds, worthless mortgages and unpaid tuition fees, into paying an arm and a leg in interest for the credit cards they had bought from this revered financial institution that had employed this upcoming BPO firm.

The familiar sinking feeling in Ardhendu's stomach overpowered him as he watched this nocturnal international drama unfold.

Manoj stretched his arms and clapped his best friend on the shoulder. "Time to split, man!"

"Only if you get rid of that idiotic, cheesy accent," said Ardhendu, his eyebrows knotted into a frown.

"It's my idiotic, cheesy bread and butter, thank you." Manoj's grin grew wider.

The harsh reality of Manoj's statement gradually sunk in. Ardhendu managed the semblance of a smile as he picked up his bag. But he couldn't help adding, "Watching you speak with that silly accent is as painful as watching Amitabh Bachchan lip sync to Shabbir Kumar's songs."

As if on cue, Manoj belted out a take-off on the singer, "Dono jawani ke masti mein chooooor, teraa koosooor na mera koosoooor…"

"Stop that!" hissed Ardhendu.

The PYTs sitting at neighbouring desks, tittered.

Ardhendu wanted to sink to the ground, but Manoj was unstoppable. Taking in the absurdity of the situation, Ardhendu grinned, then laughed shyly. Other colleagues hanging around close by joined in the merriment as the two friends walked out of the BPO together.

⟨♪⟩

The winter chill had just set in. Scores of young call centre employees swarmed around the front yard of the great Indian BPO centre — young girls in clingy tops and jeans; young guys in clingy tops and jeans.

Manoj took in the scene languidly. "You know, this is the picture of the great Indian failed models' union."

"Meaning?"

"All these lovelies have a secret desire to become another Fleur Xavier, but guess what? They end up here, working nights and dating days."

"Manoj, shush, we are assistant managers here. We need to watch our language."

"Forget that, man! They'll go out with you the moment you promise them a promotion."

"Manoj, man, stop it!"

Manoj turned around. "You don't believe me? Wait.... Hey, Ameeta!"

A PYT turned around, "Oh, hello Manoj..."

A pink top with a plunging neckline, a pair of blue jeans sprayed on, come-hither eyes, fixed squarely on Manoj — that was Ameeta.

"Listen, Ardhendu here is looking for good performers who could go to Ireland for the Knowledge Transfer Process for Cobbler's Bank. He would like to discuss this opportunity with you."

"Sure!" The come-hither eyes now moved to Ardhendu.

"At the Radisson, of course!"

"Sure!" Ameeta leaned towards Ardhendu.

"Er, not today. I'll talk to you tomorrow in the office."

"If you wish, but I am free now." She looked at him expectantly.

"Um, aah, I have to go now."

"OK." She shrugged her shoulders with an 'entirely-your-loss' look.

Manoj was enjoying the show.

Ardhendu turned to Manoj. "About time we left?"

With Ardhendu in a half run, they hurried to the parking lot where Manoj had left his motorcycle. Ardhendu hopped on the pillion.

"Don't do that crap again," he hissed into his best friend's ears.

Manoj laughed out loud.

"Man you've been dating Veena for five years now. You are gonna marry her. Think about it, you get to date just one chick in your entire miserable life. C'mon buddy, there is no harm in getting a taste of the menu on offer until then."

"Manoj, I am happy with my girl. I don't need to taste anything else."

"Man! You should have been a priest!" Manoj burst into laughter. Easy, infectious laughter. Ardhendu couldn't help but join in. Then he plugged in the iPod's earphones and Kishore Kumar's mellifluous voice sang out loud and clear, wishing for the sleep fairy to enter a house and snuggle in with the little child inside; reassuring that the sleep fairy would not discriminate between the rich and the poor and would visit all homes..."Rasta dekhe tera, vyakul man mera, yeh khoye khoye naina, yeh lambi kaali raina, aaja re neendiya..." The song, a childhood favourite, was from the Rajesh Khanna starrer *Humshakal*...

Ardhendu felt tears welling up in his eyes. Years ago, when he was an infant, a man with a clear and deep voice would sing him to sleep. His would be the last voice that Ardhendu would hear before drifting away — clear, mellifluous, loving. Ardhendu could no longer remember what the man looked like, but his voice still lingered in his head. As Kishore Kumar sang, that man seemed to be singing to Ardhendu again…

"When did you say your father built this house?"

Ardhendu shook himself out of his reverie. Manoj and he were already in Safdarjung Enclave in front of the brick-coloured building where Ardhendu lived. Ardhendu got off the motorcycle. The two friends paused a bit as Manoj lit a cigarette and repeated his question.

"When did you say your father built this house?"

"1985. Just before Dad married Mom and left for the US. Grandfather had bought the land here in the sixties at a throwaway price. Thank God for that."

"Didn't you say that your father was a doctor?"

"Yeah. He got his doctorate in Medicine from the University of Kansas."

"What really happened to him?"

Ardhendu paused for a bit, gazing up at the *barsati* where he lived with his mother. They had rented out the first and ground floors. The money came in handy and was a welcome add-on to Anjali Bose's earnings as a professor of Applied Psychology at Delhi University.

"I was just five then. And we were in Kansas City, Kansas. One evening, he came home earlier than usual. He told Mom very calmly that he might be losing his job. Within a few days he packed us off to India. So Mom and I returned to Delhi. He was to join us soon, but then…" Ardhendu drifted.

Anjali Bose had just prepared his glass of milk. She was sitting at the table cajoling him to drink it. Little Ardhendu kept shaking his head stubbornly. This was a daily ritual played to perfection by both mother and son till the former feigned anger and the latter submitted to her entreaties.

Then the phone rang.

Mom answered, then became very quiet, her fingers twirling the chord anxiously. Ardhendu heard the voice crackling over the phone. It was loud and American. "Mrs. Bose, we are sorry. There was an accident, a fire. Your husband perished in it. He was a wonderful employee and we are sending an additional $100,000 as payment for the patent he had developed..."

Mom noticed the sudden change of expression on her infant son's face and hurriedly disconnected the line. She came running towards him and threw her arms around him.

"What's happened to Daddy, Mommy?"

His mother gently kissed his eyes.

"Ardhu, when God loves someone a lot, he wants that person to be with him."

The infant looked at his mother with uncomprehending eyes.

"Daddy has gone to God, son. He is now a star in the sky."

"What is that, Mom?"

Anjali Bose lifted her son in her arms and took him out to the balcony of their flat. Darkness was slowly settling on the city and all Ardhendu could see was the jagged skyline of the buildings in the neighbourhood. Then his mother pointed to the sky and said, "See that star? That's Daddy. For your entire life, he will look after you from there."

The North Star gazed down at them benevolently.

✍

"Earth to moon rocket. Are you receiving me?" Manoj spoke into his raised fist.

Ardhendu returned to earth. "Explorers on the moon, Tintin," observed Ardhendu.

"Bingo!" said Manoj.

Ardhendu smiled. "I have a lot to thank you for. You used to loan me money when we were in school…"

"Yeah? You borrowed fifty bucks from me in the twelfth standard to take Veena out for your first date…if I add fifteen per cent interest per annum…wait a minute, you owe me five hundred and fifty rupees."

Ardhendu rolled his eyes.

"Aur agar tune mujhe woh paise nahin lautaye, to main tujhe zinda nahin chodunga, jaan se maardunga!" This was Manoj mimicking Shatrughan Sinha.

"Once a *marwari*, always a *marwari*…"

"Yeah, I know, but we still get all the Bengali chicks in Calcutta because of the condition of the young unmarried Bengali male." Manoj was doing a Dev Anand this time.

"And what's that?"

"You mean, you don't know what the condition of a young Bengali unmarried male is?" Manoj asked in mock alarm.

"What?"

"Quaid mein hain bulbul!" Manoj switched to the Mithun Chakraborty mode now.

The two broke into hearty guffaws. Manoj winked at his friend, convinced that he had made Ardhendu feel better, at least for the day. Then he kick-started the motorcycle and drove off.

Ardhendu ran up the stairs and slid in the key. As he stepped into the flat, Crystal, the Labrador who had been with him for almost six years now, yelped with joy and jumped on him, before running back to the door and thumping it with its paws.

"OK girl. I get it. Follow me."

He opened the door and ran downstairs, Crystal bounding behind him. Together, they dashed off to the park right behind the house. Crystal went round and round in a frenzy, then finding a discreet corner, relieved herself. Free from her burden now, she sniffed the relatively pure, CNG-fed, Delhi morning air before breaking into another mindless run.

Ardhendu sat on the bench watching the flurry of Crystal's feet, her ears pushed back like wings, her tail wagging in the air like a chopper's blades as she dashed from one end of the park to the other.

"She's pretty, isn't she?"

It was Mr. Gupta. Like the Phantom of Indrajal Comics, this bearded, tall and middle-aged man, crept up behind Ardhendu's back from nowhere. Ardhendu almost jumped out of his skin! Then turning around wearily, he gazed at the man in his jogging suit, his face covered by a sinister hood.

It was still dark. Mars was bright in the sky, almost like a cricket ball. The sky was clear, the air crisp, and the early winter breeze, refreshingly cold. Ardhendu pulled his jacket around him tighter. He whistled to Crystal, who came bounding to him, and jumped all over Mr. Gupta. Ardhendu looked wearily at Crystal and wondered if she would ever be capable of hostility in her life. Perhaps she would greet a burglar at their home in the same way.

Mr. Gupta who was on his morning walk, his beard even thicker today, asked, "So, young man, how have you been?"

"Er, fine, Sir…" Ardhendu responded.

"Good," Mr. Gupta said, and marched out of the park.

Ardhendu wondered about this man. He would see him most mornings in the park, walking or even jogging. He hardly spoke to anyone, but always had a kind word for Ardhendu. Where did Mr. Gupta live? In which block? What did he do? Did he have a family?

Then realisation dawned on Ardhendu: during all these years of bumping into Mr. Gupta in the park, not once had Ardhendu bothered to ask him anything about himself. Was that a good thing or a bad thing? Had he been discreet or plain indifferent? Ardhendu shook his head in dismay. Why was he so cut off from the rest of the world? Why did people not interest him? Why couldn't he be like other guys? Was he really nothing but a selfish, good-for-nothing city slicker?

His spirits dipped a few notches at these thoughts and suddenly he felt tired. So he whistled at Crystal, then turned around and walked back to the flat, the faithful canine at his heels.

Anjali Bose was up by the time they returned. A steaming mug of tea awaited him.

"So how was your day...er, night?"

Ardhendu did not respond.

"You OK, son?"

He kept quiet.

Anjali recognised that trait. He had inherited it from his father. Whenever Amitava Bose was troubled, he would retreat into that little cave in his mind. Getting him out of there was always an arduous task and the cause for many an argument young Anjali would have with the only man she had ever loved. But with her son, it was different. She could bully him. She was the mother after all.

"OK, out with it!"

"Out with what?"

"With whatever ails thee!"

"Oh, nothing, Mom."

"Ardhu..."

Ardhendu looked up at his mother. Memories of a couple of resounding slaps that helped raise a good child came back to him.

He smiled. And sighed. The tea had warmed him by now. Looking out of the window of the dining room, he could see that Crystal had settled down on the rug in the balcony.

"I am tired of this silly job, Mom."

Anjali said nothing. She just did not want to interrupt her son.

"I didn't get this MBA to work in a sweat shop, at a call centre. This experience is not going to help me. I want to work with a good IT or pharmaceutical company, in its operations stream. I want to rise in that stream to become a CEO some day. Here, I am simply rotting away."

Anjali listened patiently.

"So what's really stopping you from applying to some good companies?"

"My degree, Mom!" Ardhendu blurted out. "All the good IT and pharmaceutical companies hire management graduates from the top five management institutes. Gokul Chand is not even in the top two hundred. So where do I go from here?"

Anjali sighed. She could feel her patience ebb. "Why are we going over this again? You know we never had that kind of money to send you to the Indian School of Business, or abroad, for that matter."

"Mom, I was born in the US. I am an American citizen. You could have worked something out."

The dam burst. Anjali's eyes blazed. She began to smart at her son's barb. "Yes, I could have, had you studied hard and scored 700 in your GMAT. But no, you scored only around 450. Which university would have given you a scholarship with that kind of a score?"

"But Mom, that's the best I could do…"

Anjali did not let him finish. She got up from her chair and shot back, "No! That is not the best you *could have* done. The best you ever did was to hang on to the pallu of that girl…"

This time, Ardhendu did not let her finish: "That's a hell of a thing to say, Mom…"

But, Anjali was not going to be cowed down: "No, that's not a hell of a thing to say. The truth is, Ardhendu Bose, you have such low self-esteem that you thought that the best you could do is bag that girl. Also, the truth is that this girl has made you believe that the best you could do was Gokul Chand Institute of Management. Why? Because anything beyond that and she would have lost you to someone better. So she fed your low self-esteem and weaknesses, making you believe that the only world you have is in her arms…"

By now Ardhendu's ears were burning. He couldn't take it anymore. "Mom, that's enough!"

"Yes. That's enough. Someday you'll realise that's also the truth," Anjali bit her tongue in time to stop herself from saying *"that you could never be a real man. Like your father!"*

She walked away to her bedroom in a huff. She had to get ready for class. "Don't forget your breakfast." She called out before getting into the bathroom.

Ardhendu sat sullenly at the dining table. The morning sky began to lighten with the first rays of the sun. It was a bright new day. But for him, it was just another night.

∽

Before setting out for the day, Anjali peeped into her son's room. Ardhendu slept peacefully on his bed, his arms around the cuddly Crystal who moved her head gently in acknowledgement so as to not wake her master. Anjali smiled at Crystal, then pulling out another blanket, she gently covered both. Turning the regulator of the fan to low, she stole a quick look at her boy. She felt the need to apologise. A wave of guilt swept over her. What she had just subjected him to? After all, he was the one who had to grow up without a father. She wanted to speak to him, hold him to her breast, make him feel secure, but he was fast asleep. She turned around and slipped out of the flat, letting the latch of the door fasten behind her quietly.

As she drove towards Delhi University, she made a silent wish: "May all his dreams come true!"

3

Ardhendu tried to talk to the girl at the desk with whatever dignity he still had, to get her interested in his resumé. But she just waved him away. "Leave it on the desk and we'll call you if we have something."

The guys behind him surged forward, so he had to move away quickly. He watched them sing the same tune he had to the girl, for whom it was just another day of getting yet another bunch of hopefuls out of her way. Slowly, he made his way out of the hallway of the seedy Nehru Place building. He read the sign one last time: PCM Consultants: Building Careers!

Each time he had seen their ad in a newspaper, he had emailed his resumé to them, but never got a response. So this time, he had decided to go himself. Now he wished he hadn't. Scores of young MBAs had cropped up in this city, graduating from nondescript MBA schools that had paid off various governmental agencies to make a buck for themselves out of unsuspecting fools. In a country of a billion, perhaps, a million wanted to be MBAs, and these schools would slake the thirst. But the top companies did not want the wretched lot passing out from here. They were looking for pedigree! The US was coming out of recession; Europe was in a mess; Iceland and Greece had collapsed. The multinationals in India hired only from the best. The rest, like him, went to sweat shops on walk-in-45° C sales jobs.

Ardhendu felt a sense of shame as he shuffled out, pulling his jacket closer to keep out the foggy chill. The cold International Trade Tower with its adjacent hotel, the flyover ahead of him, the innumerable cars rolling on crowded lanes, trying to get ahead of each other — almost everything had taken on the grey of the sky. The fog was slowly lifting, but the Delhi chill kept digging into his bones. He crossed the road and hailed an auto rickshaw. He needed to get home soon and sleep before his night shift. He looked at his watch. It was already 11.30 am. At least Mom wouldn't be home to ask embarrassing questions today.

He got into the auto rickshaw, taking in the dull noise of the auto's engine, the incessant honking of the cars, the exasperated looks on the drivers' faces, the vehicles running neck to neck on the Ring Road... He wanted to run away...from it all. He shut his eyes and plugged his ears with his hands, sinking his face deep into his chest, shutting the world out. But the more he tried to do that, the more it bounced right back, until he felt that if he would jump out of the auto rickshaw into the path of an oncoming truck, it would be a quick end. Declared spot dead. By then the auto rickshaw was on the IIT flyover. The noise settled a bit as the rooftops of South Delhi whizzed past Ardhendu's range of vision. He was fifteen minutes from home and the comfort of his bed. Suddenly, home seemed more appealing. Bi-polar? Schizophrenic? No, no. All humans must have felt this way at least once in a lifetime. At least once. Ardhendu firmly put all suicidal thoughts out of his mind. The auto rickshaw climbed down from the flyover and turned right after the Deer Park, its racket continuing as it swept in and out of Safdarjung Enclave's by lanes, emerging out on the side of the Matri Mandir.

The sight of the Matri Mandir stirred the Bengali in Ardhendu. So he asked the auto rickshaw driver to pull up on the side. Then he got off, removed his shoes and went inside to pray. The serene eyes of the head priest, Acharya Mukul Mukherjee took him in as he entered the temple of the Goddess.

"Bhalo achho?" he asked as he offered him some pooja flowers. *"Boudi bhalo achhen?"*

"Hain, Ma bhalo achhe," Ardhendu replied, marvelling at how the Acharya always referred to his mother with the Bengali honorific *'Boudi'* (sister-in-law).

"Poojo te ebaar Amit Kumar aashchhen," the priest said, his kind eyes full of warmth for this boy whom he had seen in the temple from the time he was knee-high.

Ardhendu's eyes widened. "Amit Kumar? He is going to perform here during Durga Poojo?"

"Yes, absolutely," the priest replied in English, aware of Ardhendu's love for the singer's father. The Acharya had sensed the sadness in the boy's eyes and had decided to cheer him up a bit. The brief smile in Ardhendu's eyes told him that he had succeeded. Ardhendu was stumped by the Acharya's flawless English.

"He's done his doctorate in Theology from Delhi University," Mom had told to him some years ago, almost challenging him to do one.

The momentary joy he had felt about the opportunity to watch Kishore Kumar's son live, disappeared. *"Achcha, choli."*

He bid the Acharya goodbye. From the stoop in his gait as he walked out, the Acharya understood that the melancholy that had brought the boy to the temple had not gone away. He sighed as he went back to his duties, and added a prayer for the boy's well-being to the Divine Mother.

Back home, Ardhendu brushed his teeth, ate a boiled egg and a toast, showered, and got into bed, Crystal adding warmth and comfort. He dozed off, keeping his phone on silent. No, he didn't feel like talking today, not even to Veena.

When he woke, he found Anjali holding his face in her hands, *"Ki hoechhe re?"* she asked, her eyes full of maternal warmth and concern. *"Shopno dekhechhish?"*

For a second, Ardhendu did not register anything, and then he realised her hands were wet...from the tears that had fallen from his eyes in his sleep.

"If you resist what is happening to you, it will keep coming back to you. You need to accept, no, actually choose what you have now, Ardhu. Only then will it stop coming back to you. Accept Ardhu, and do your best!"

Ardhendu hugged his mother. This time he did not try to hold back the tears that streamed down his cheeks in torrents. Nor did it matter that he was twenty-three.

$\backsim$

Three weeks later, on a Monday morning, Manoj called out to Ardhendu who had just finished processing a call in a neighbouring work-station.

"What is it?" Ardhendu asked as Manoj shoved a copy of Wednesday's *Ascent* under his nose.

"Read it, you dork."

Ardhendu shook his head. He was in the middle of his shift. He had got a spot award from the shift head, and the HR guys who worked day shifts had come in that night. They made a song and dance about how this team had won the Belfast contract for their client's credit card processing project. This was followed by a mail from the CEO about how they had now crossed $150 million in revenues. The bottom line was that they had to get the Knowledge Transfer Process done this month. A team was to be dispatched to Northern Ireland with the client to understand the data. They had just about 30 days to do a live demo.

Ardhendu was wondering how on earth he would get all this work done with five of his team members already having put in their papers. He had sought the HR manager's help for the task at hand and was reading his response. It had been ccd to his boss and several other people to ensure that the HR manager's behind was sufficiently covered.

Dear Ardhendu,

As you know, we are business partners to you; however, retention is entirely your responsibility! We would like to know why is it that this project team's attrition has hit 15%? Please send a detailed report on the analytics following which you will be contacted accordingly.

Ardhendu looked at the word 'accordingly'; what did that mean? What was the meaning of all this meaningless jargon — 'accordingly', 'seemingly', 'as discussed'? What use were these words to business communication, he wondered… He waved Manoj away. The last thing he needed right now were his wisecracks.

Manoj stood his ground. "Read this, you ass!"

Ardhendu was ready to do anything to get rid of Manoj at that moment. So he snatched the newspaper and stared at it. 'We are looking for Management Trainees.' Below that, was an unmistakable logo: RED. And below that, was an email ID. That was it! Ardhendu stared at the ad. It was a half-pager. "They're here in India?"

"Made an announcement on CNBC last week. Said that they were kicking off their largest Research & Development lab with an office in Delhi."

Ardhendu couldn't believe his eyes... RED was the fourth largest Life Sciences company in the world! What were they doing here in India, more so, placing an ad for management trainees? He looked at the page for a few seconds and then set it aside.

Manoj grabbed him by the shoulder. "You're still gonna be an idiot?"

Suddenly it struck Ardhendu that Manoj had finally got the hang of the American accent he had found so irritating: the false Khs for Ks, the incessant rolls of Rs, the naats for the nots, the hays for the heys... He smiled for a brief second. "Forget it, we don't stand a chance."

"Why not?" Manoj quipped back. "It doesn't say you have to be from a premier university and all that crap. Just says that they need management trainees."

Manoj had his best friend's attention. He wasn't going to give up that easily. "C'mon, let's apply!"

Ardhendu was not convinced. "Why would they place an ad? They are one of the world's top four Life Sciences companies They just need to spread the word around and the IIM/XLRI guys would follow them in a neat Pied Piper-file."

"Yeah, I know, but what do we have to lose? C'mon, let's apply."

"You're sure it's not a franchise, or something?"

"Shut up, Ardhu. Just apply."

Manoj grabbed Ardhendu by his arm and dragged him across the hall. A couple of PYTs looked up from their desks, eyebrows raised. Ardhendu smiled almost apologetically at them. The two friends headed straight for the library for one of the stand-alone PCs with internet connections. Manoj went into his Yahoo mail account and dashed off his resumé. Then Ardhendu did the same.

"Here we go. Nothing to lose," he thought.

Then they looked at each other and grinned.

✐

Ardhendu sat in the reception area of the spanking new office at Connaught Place. He had put on his only suit bought off a clearance sale, two summers ago.

A few young men and women sat ahead of him waiting to be interviewed. The PYT at the reception had told him that she was part of the contractual staff employed with the temp services firm engaged by RED. The sense of professionalism in the room was unmistakable. The receptionist's demeanour was polite, and professional and all the candidates who had been called for the interviews were treated well.

Ardhendu gratefully accepted the receptionist's offer for a beverage. A uniformed attendant appeared from nowhere with a pot of Brazilian coffee. It was served in fine bone china. He sipped gratefully, marvelling at the rich texture of the brew. Beautiful and expensive art adorned the mahogany walls all around, and the décor in light orange and dark red accentuated the impeccable mark of taste in the reception area. On the wall behind the receptionist was subtly displayed a logo: RED.

Ardhendu prayed silently to God. Two other IIT/IIM guys sat ahead of him. Shuffling his feet and wringing his fingers nervously, he straightened his tie and waited. If only he would get a chance. One of the IIT/IIM types was called inside, and he sauntered past Ardhendu with an unmistakable air of authority and confidence. Ardhendu looked at him in awe and envy. How different would it have been if he too had that air of authority, that sense of confidence, that intellectually arrogant look, that fine suit, the knowledge and yes, that degree? The old familiar sinking feeling in the stomach invaded Ardhendu once again. He was sure that the guy who had just gone in would walk away with the job.

Suddenly, Ardhendu felt the need to get up and leave. He knew he would be ridiculed during the interview. They would politely tell him, as had many others in the past, "We'll get back to you." That seemingly benevolent look, with those cold sneering eyes; the look several interviewers had given him over the past few months. He couldn't take it anymore. He wanted to run away, escape from it all. He felt very angry with Manoj. If it weren't for that buck-toothed bastard, he wouldn't be here today. He wouldn't have to put up with this ignominy, this bitter, shameful, terrible feeling of rejection! And where the hell was Manoj today? Hadn't he been called for an interview?

The temp wasn't looking at Ardhendu, so he got up and slowly edged his way out of the open door, out of the hallway. Without looking back, he broke into a half-walk, half-run, down the stairs and, before he knew, he was out of the building.

The milling crowd at Connaught Place, went about their business, with nary a care for him. He was thirsty, very thirsty. So he stopped by a roadside shop and ordered a cola. He drank deeply from the bottle. The cola did not slake his thirst.

He asked for one of those new real lemon drinks. As he took his first sip, he realised that he was no longer so thirsty. He should have waited for the cola to take effect. That was a waste of money. Then with the drink in hand, he moved to a nearby tree, trying to avoid the second-hand smoke blown out by all those outlaws that willfully disobeyed the health minister's diktat.

He sipped slowly, relieved to be away from that office, relieved not to have gone through the interview. Slowly, his head cleared. The winter air was welcoming. He took another sip, enjoying the breeze and then from the corner of his eye, he saw him. The IIT/IIM guy! He was walking out from that building, his head bent low, the veneer of arrogance completely gone from him. It was unmistakable, that look of dejection, shame and rejection! The guy walked slowly and heavily. On an impulse, Ardhendu walked up to him. He touched him briefly on his sleeve. The guy looked around, recognition writ on his face. "Weren't you upstairs…"

"Yes, I was. How did it go?"

"Weird! They wound up in ten minutes. They told me that I wouldn't suit the role. It was all very abrupt. I wonder what they are looking for…" he drifted off, all zest gone from him now, and then asked, "Is your name Ardhendu Bose?"

"Yes, how did you know?"

"The receptionist was asking for you."

Ardhendu did not wait to hear more. He turned back and ran as fast as he could back into the building, up the stairs, into the room, panting heavily. His life seemed to be rewinding.

The receptionist looked up at him, a big smile on her face. "Where were you? Ramesh asked at least thrice for you!"

Ardhendu made a few noises at having had to make a call and all that.

"Please go in, he's waiting for you!" she said, in that perfect, sing-song voice that receptionists are trained to have.

Ardhendu did just that.

⌒

It was a tastefully decorated room, something one saw in Hollywood films on royalty. A lone gentleman in a tie sat behind a plush table, with his jacket slung over his chair. On his table sat a small laptop and Ardhendu's resumé.

"Hi, I am Ramesh Tyagi. I head the Delhi chapter of Arms International Consultants. We are RED's global partners in talent search and retention. We are helping them set up their India operations."

Ardhendu shook the offered hand firmly and sat down.

"So Ardhendu, tell me a little about yourself."

The interview took an hour. Ardhendu marvelled at the way Ramesh put him at ease and extracted every bit of information about him. He ended up sharing every possible detail about himself, his education, work and his family, and Crystal! Once Ardhendu had finished speaking, Ramesh looked at him. Then he looked again at the resumé held in his neatly manicured hand, and asked softly, "Would you like to think about this or should we move ahead?"

For a moment Ardhendu was too stunned to reply. He could not believe his ears. Then restraining himself so as not to sound too eager, he said politely, "I think that should be fine. We can move ahead."

"Good!" said Ramesh. "We don't believe in wasting time. Among many of the open positions that we currently have in India, there is one which I think you would fit — Executive Assistant to President, India Operations, RED."

Ardhendu sank into his richly upholstered chair. He was trying to digest what he had just been told; a management trainee position in operations is the best that he had hoped for. Being an executive assistant to the President of India, Operations would actually mean building, reviewing and tracking all operations parameters from thought to implementation, being part of business planning, budgeting, human resources forecasting, tracking, costing and coordinating review mechanisms.

In short, he would learn everything about operations! This was the dream job he had been looking for!

Suddenly he went numb. They were choosing him. Him, over the premier institute guys! Had he heard right? He stared at Ramesh waiting for him to say something that would break the spell.

Ramesh's sharp head-hunting eyes observed him closely. Reading his mind clearly, he smiled reassuringly. Then almost conspiratorially, he leaned forward, his voice going down a few octaves. "Between you and me, I don't really care much for those premier institute types. It's only hands-on people who can execute. RED does not have much need for the PowerPoint prima donnas."

Ardhendu was about to agree, but then decided that discretion was better than valour. So he just returned a faint smile.

"Well, then, the next steps — I want you to meet Colton White, the American President of RED's India Operations. He is in tomorrow."

'Colton White' — the name inspired immediate awe in Ardhendu. It had a remote, inaccessible ring to it. 'Colton'... how very American it sounded, like the name of one of those movie stars. He marvelled at how these Americans had such cool names, while he was stuck with such a lame one. Or did their station in life lend that magical edge to their names? One way or the other, he wished he too had such a cool-sounding name like Abraham, Bill or Ronald, or better still something that sounded exotic and was popular with Indian royalty like, say, Dhananjay, Vikramaditya, or Ajatshatru…and 'Singh' was preferable to 'Bose' or was it really…

"He works US hours. Does that work for you?" Ramesh interrupted Ardhendu's train of thoughts with his rather indulgent smile.

"Yes, it does," Ardhendu replied quickly.

"OK, 8 pm sounds fine?"

Ardhendu did not know what to say, except, "Yes, of course!"

The first thing that struck Ardhendu about Colton White was his height. He stood at an impressive six feet six inches. His broad shoulders, accentuated by his well-fitted Versace suit, stood out as he got up from his table. Then he walked towards Ardhendu in long strides. Gripping Ardhendu's hand warmly, his deep blue eyes held Ardhendu in a hypnotic gaze. "Colton White." Power and strength oozed from almost every pore. Ardhendu gazed at him, speechless. The man standing in front of him looked like a Greek god; strikingly handsome, powerful, a cross between a Cary Grant and a Mel Gibson. He seemed to be in his mid-forties.

"So this is what power CEOs look like." Ardhendu's internal dialogue fed him that information. It was as if this Greek god had read his mind. Then he smiled with his mouth shut, beckoning Ardhendu to a sofa in the corner of the room. He settled down into an adjacent sofa, folded one long leg over the other comfortably. He wore ornately designed cowboy boots. Ardhendu marvelled at the brilliant handiwork. White caught him staring at the boots and smiled. "I am from Kansas, so it figures, right?" Seeing the expression of uncertainty on Ardhendu's face, he smiled again. "Contrary to popular belief, actually Kansas, not Texas, is original cowboy country. Dodge City, Kansas is where Wyatt Earp and his ilk are from. So if you are from Kansas, chances are you'll have your boots stashed away somewhere!" Then he asked Ardhendu, if he would like something to drink. He was obviously trying to put Ardhendu at ease.

"A coffee would be great."

"Sure." He turned one long arm across his table, hitting a button on his phone. "Hey Michelle, could we get some Columbian for our valued guest, please?"

A vision in a skirt and blouse appeared almost immediately. Ardhendu's jaw dropped. The sheer beauty of the blonde that walked in took his breath away. No Hollywood beauty he had seen could ever come anywhere close. That sinking feeling began in his stomach again. He began to feel very inferior. His mind began to tell him that indeed, he was in the company of a very superior race. Colton and this woman, Michelle seemed the epitome of perfection in every possible way. In sharp contrast, he seemed some sort of a low life, a wretched creature that did not deserve to be here.

Michelle gave him a dazzling smile. "Hey, how're you doing today? Would you like some milk in your coffee?"

Ardhendu stood up, tongue tied, nodding his thanks. Expertly, she made his coffee and handed it to him with a gracious smile. Then, as efficiently as she had arrived, she left, her long heels making music on the floor.

After waiting a bit for the young man to deal with his thoughts, White leaned forward. "Ardhendu, I am not going to go over the discussion you have had with Ramesh. That is done. Let me tell you about RED's India strategy." He strode up to his table, clicked on his laptop and a screen came alive behind him with the RED logo and a corporate film. Suddenly it seemed as though a hundred violinists had taken over the room as the music flowed from the high-definition speakers around him. Ardhendu watched, fascinated.

"RED corporation, the world's fourth largest Life Sciences company!" said a voiceover.

Stunning visuals followed, showcasing the company's presence in the USA, Europe, Canada and Australia. Its ground-breaking research work and patented medicines for blood-related diseases flashed across the screen: *a vaccine for tuberculosis, a preventive medicine for malaria, oral pills for controlling thalassemia, drug development for anemia and its ground-breaking research work for developing active mutating antibodies to battle HIV and AIDS...* pioneering and award-winning work done by this progressive organisation.

Some of the world's finest scientists were employed by RED that also sponsored research by universities like Harvard, MIT, etc.

The final visuals were that of New Delhi, with the voiceover booming: "Our final frontier — Asia and notably, India! The land of the finest doctors and research talent. RED will open its world's largest Research & Development lab in India, from where the next generation mutating medicinal drugs will be developed!"

And then the screen went blank.

Ardhendu was mesmerised.

White strode back to the sofa and looked earnestly at Ardhendu. "We are in negotiation with the Indian government for a unique R&D project." He sat down, paused, turned around and asked, "Would you like a drink?"

"Er, um, here?" asked Ardhendu hesitantly.

White chuckled to himself. "I am told that this is against the Indian office culture, but it is fine in parts of the West, especially Europe. Anyway, I work nights, so having a drink or two doesn't really matter. Tell me your preference. Whisky?"

Keen not to offend, Ardhendu nodded.

White got up and went over to a small cabinet behind his table. He pressed a button which opened up a swivel bar, pulled out a bottle of Bunnahabhain 18 years, poured two shots in malt glasses and strode across the room. Offering one to Ardhendu, he sniffed his drink carefully before taking a sip. Rolling the single malt in his mouth, he swallowed slowly. "Low peat, unlike regular Islay malt. An initial explosion on the palate, followed by a warming finish. The notes are fresh, sweet, sea air, firm body and a full finish. Excellent, indeed!"

White's comments on the whisky's finer points were Hebrew to Ardhendu. He tasted the malt gingerly, its strength hitting him with full force. As he swallowed, he had a coughing fit as though he had swallowed an erupting volcano.

White clapped him gently on the back. "Are you OK?"

"Ah, yes Sir... Sorry."

"Oh don't worry young man. Single malt is like that for the first time. You'll get used to it...

"So, coming back to where we had left off, we have offered a unique project to the government and with the Games round the corner, they should be happy to consider it: a city like Delhi has thousands of homeless, impoverished people. We would like to take responsibility for at least a thousand such people. We have bought some land in Uttaranchal where we plan to build our R&D lab. Every year, we will take in a thousand or more such homeless people, pay for their healthcare, food, education and rehabilitation. We will provide them with vocational knowledge and basic education. When they leave the lab, they will be able to find some meaningful occupation. In return, we are asking the government to allow us to carry out initial testing of our new drugs on them."

"Testing?" Ardhendu asked.

"Yes. These people are denied basic healthcare. Many of the infants are not even inoculated when they are born. They carry various forms of blood-related diseases. We will take samples from them regularly and treat them with our world-class healthcare systems. In return, we will test our new drugs on them in a very safe and clinical environment. Our scientists will be there round the clock to monitor their health. After a year, we will send them back to Delhi, where they will be rehabilitated. We have extensive corporate social responsibility programmes, which we wish to also introduce and many of these people would ultimately find employment under those programmes."

"That's a noble purpose, but what does RED get in return for this enormous investment?"

"Good question, Ardhendu. Governments in the US and Europe do not allow human trials like this on such a scale. We are on the verge of some major discoveries. Think, an HIV vaccine, cure for AIDS, eradication of tuberculosis. We have developed fabulous cocktail drugs for these. All we need is the permission of governments to carry out large scale human testing.

"India is a country with a high concentration of blood-related cases — 2.5 million HIV cases, 1 million malaria cases, chronic tuberculosis cases…the list is endless. If the government gives us this opportunity, think of the kind of medical breakthrough this world will have. We will manufacture these drugs here in India and market them across the world.

"Think, Ardhendu, ground-breaking medical drugs developed here in India, a low-cost manufacturing country. The world will have access to these drugs at such affordable rates! The FDA can take fifteen years to certify a drug. If we can complete the human testing of all these drugs here, we can apply for those patents quickly!"

Ardhendu was spellbound. White's deep blue eyes burnt bright with a passionate fire. White, White, burning bright; in the dark of the night…

"And you, Ardhendu, will be part of the team that builds this transformation."

White stood up. He extended his hand. "Come, join RED."

Ardhendu stood up smartly and clasped the offered hand firmly.

"Of course, Sir. Tell me when?"

"As soon as you can get out of your notice period. You will start off as my executive assistant and I will build you a fantastic career. Ramesh will meet you after this and work out a compensation package." Then he paused, clasping his hands. "May I ask you a personal question? This would probably be an illegal question in the US, so I apologise in advance. Were you at any time related to a gentleman called Amitava Bose? Dr. Amitava Bose?"

Ardhendu's face lit up. "Yes, of course! He was my father!"

White stared at him intently on hearing the answer, and his expression changed to that of deep respect.

"This is amazing! Just, truly amazing!"

"Why is that?"

"Your father was one of the most brilliant doctors I have had the privilege of knowing!"

Ardhendu was puzzled for a while.

White's forehead crinkled. The deep blue eyes seemed to glisten momentarily. "I have had the privilege of working very closely with him; this was before he passed away, of course."

Ardhendu was pleasantly surprised. His memories of his father were very sketchy. In fact, other than a couple of photographs, he didn't remember much of him. All that remained with him was a blurred image of a strong man with a deep voice and an unexplained feeling of love.

"We were earlier called Rochester Edwards Corporation. Your father worked for the Mount Carmel group of hospitals that had a very well-respected research arm. We had bought that over in the eighties. Post that acquisition, he became an employee. He was a brilliant man. Did some path-breaking, phenomenal research for us until that lab fire..." White broke off. His mind seemed to be far away... Then he turned around, and shaking his head, said, "I am sorry. He was such a brilliant man. It must have been hard for you and your mother..."

Ardhendu still did not know what to say. All this was happening a bit too fast.

"Listen, Ardhendu, it is going to be an absolute privilege to have the late Dr. Bose's son working with us. Please do come on board quickly!"

"Yes, Sir, of course!" said Ardhendu, overwhelmed.

"Any questions?" White asked, politely.

"Er, yes."

"Go ahead."

"Is RED a synonym for Rochester Edwards Corporation?"

"Well, that wasn't really rocket science," he said with a half-smile. "We respected the companies that we acquired. But it was too much to continue with our original name, so we decided to shorten it as much as possible and keep a kind of a logo."

"Oh, I see," Ardhendu responded, nodding his head quite sagely.

Suddenly, White shot him a piercing glance. His thin lips smiled ever so briefly. "But that is not the truth." White's voice took on a sinister edge. He spoke in a low octave, as he leaned closer to Ardhendu. "You want to know the truth?"

Ardhendu nodded, stupefied.

"We deal with blood-related diseases, right?"

"Er, yes," said Ardhendu, unnerved at the sudden turn of White's demeanour.

"And the colour of blood is?"

"RED...?"

"Exactly." White hissed, like a Machiavellian villain.

Ardhendu managed a faint smile. White's deep blue eyes seemed to read Ardhendu's mind...and then, he broke into a loud guffaw!

"I'm just teasing you man!" He laughed, while clapping him on his back. "It's nothing like that! Welcome aboard, Mr. Bose! Look forward to a long and fruitful association!" White's laughter was infectious... Ardhendu got the joke and burst into laughter himself. Then he downed the rest of the single malt in a swift gulp, and headed for the door that led out of Colton White's chamber. Suddenly he realised that he had forgotten to thank his host for his hospitality. So he stopped in his tracks and turned about like a Kirov Ballet artiste before noticing that the room was empty. Colton White had disappeared. And the swivel bar was shut.

The two used crystal glasses, however, still lay on the tables next to the sofas.

Ardhendu stepped out, shutting the fancy door behind him noiselessly.

Red, red, dread, dead...Mephisto pounding away in his head.

But Ardhendu had no reason to feel anything but elated.

That night he drifted off to sleep, holding comfortably on to Crystal. He marvelled at the turn of events of the day. His inner voice told him that things were working out, at last! And as he completed one cycle of his rapid eye movement, he thanked the man who he had thought of at times, for so many years of his life.

"Thanks, Dad," he said aloud, before the coziness of the room goaded him off to sleep.

Of all people, he dreamt of Mr Gupta that night.

"So, young man, still with that BPO company?"

"Well Sir, actually I'm leaving it."

"Where are you going?"

"Well, it's a multinational called RED."

"That American Life Sciences company? Did you read the small print in your letter?"

"No, why?"

"Well it's a multinational, they may have different policies that may not be suited to the Indian environment. They may also fire at will. Don't you think you should work in a good established Indian organisation?"

"Don't worry, Uncle. No one wants to work for those stodgy Indian companies anymore. It's the multinationals that we Generation Ys want a piece of!"

"Well yes, young man but remember, the world is in the midst of an economic turmoil. Most markets in the West are already saturated. India has the distinct advantage of a fast-growing population which fuels the internal demand, much of which has faded in Western countries as their population is actually ageing. The largest group of people in any country under the age of thirty, actually resides in this land. An Indian company whose primary market is in India would have much more stability and knowledge of this market. You must look before you leap or else you may be in a deep well."

Ardhendu suddenly woke up from the dream trying to decode it, then fell back into deep slumber.

4

They sat at their old college canteen.

"So tell me, what do you have in mind?" asked Veena.

Ardhendu smiled. "This is where we used to meet in college, do you remember?"

Veena looked around and smiled, her pearly teeth gleaming in the afternoon sun that filtered through the open window.

Two coke bottles cast shadows on their table.

"Veena, I got the job!"

Veena's grin broadened. "Congrats, sweetheart!"

"They are offering me a starting salary of fifteen lakh rupees a year. Plus US stock options. Do you know what that means? In six months, I become eligible for annual leave. Then I'll take you on a cruise for our honeymoon."

"Canary Islands?"

"Greek Islands!"

Veena reached out her hand and closed her palm over Ardhendu's. He quickly freed himself and shoved something into her hand. She looked at it, her eyes opening wide...a diamond ring.

"And, here's my wedding gift for the two love birds!" Manoj arrived from nowhere, two lottery tickets in hand. "A crore each, kiddos!"

"A crore, huh? Your generosity knows no bounds!" Ardhendu laughed softly.

"You bet! Now go and enjoy yourselves!"

The two got up and began to walk out of the canteen.

"Hey, wait a sec!" Manoj called out.

They turned around.

"What if you really win the lottery?"

༄

A beautiful benarasi sari awaited Anjali Bose as she stepped into the flat. "So you got the job, huh? RED is Rochester Edwards? I didn't know that," Anjali said as she picked up his clothes from the floor."

"Yes, Mom. I start off with fifteen lakhs per year."

Anjali turned around in surprise.

"And you get around three lakhs now?"

"Yes, Mom," Ardhendu said with pride.

"Is there a catch somewhere?"

Ardhendu put his arms around his mother. "Mauuum!"

Anjali smiled, genuinely happy for her son. "It's a very good company, son. They took very good care of your father. They ensured that all that was due to him reached me after he... [she didn't like using the words 'passed away']. He really liked working there in the beginning, but towards the end... well, I think he became keen to start his own practice. So he began to find fault with his new boss. I think it had more to do with your father's dominating nature than anything his boss had actually done."

Ardhendu thought he'd update his mother about the fact that he was reporting to the same man, but decided against it.

"It's a low profile organisation, but has excellent people practices. It's a very well-known company, son. With revenues of fifty billion dollars, it is a well-respected Fortune 500 company. You must work hard there."

"I will, Mom."

Ardhendu stood around wanting to say something. Anjali noticed this as she shoved his clothes and soiled underwear into the old washing machine that they owned. She shook her head.

"It's about Veena, right?"

"Yes, Mom. We plan on getting married in May."

"You're an adult, Ardhendu. It's your choice." Anjali seemed to be pouting.

"C'mon, Mom. Can't you be happy for me?"

Anjali sighed. She set the timer on the machine and pressed the start button. Satisfied that this chore was done, she turned around and finally faced her son. "Yes, I can. But that girl erodes your basic assertion. You are so dependent on her. You can never come into your own as long as you have her with you. Ardhu, you need to be assertive and self-dependent..."

"Mom, please, not today. Can you be happy for me? Once?"

Anjali bit her lip and tried to wipe away the frown on her face. Then she smiled weakly, and kissing Ardhendu on his forehead, she muttered, "He would have been proud of you..."

5

It was his first day at RED. The mobile rang. He looked at it for a moment and guilt overtook him. He let it ring for a few seconds and then picked it up gingerly.

"Mr. Bond!" Manoj's voice rang out with a cheery fake British accent. "This is M. Nay, not Moneypenny. All the best, for your new mission!"

Ardhendu couldn't help but marvel at how Manoj managed to keep his cheer even in the face of continuing loss.

"*It's about changing your paradigm.*" He would say. "*A situation is exactly what you make of it...you call it lousy, it appears lousy. You call it good, it appears good...*"

"Mr. Bond...?" Manoj queried, "up in the clouds again, Mr. Bond?"

Ardhendu came back to earth.

"I'm sorry...thanks, man. I am sorry they didn't call you..."

"Doesn't matter. You, me, it's all the same! Go show them what you're worth."

"Manoj, you've always been a good friend…"

"Shut up and head down!" Manoj meant it. He disconnected his phone, and smiled to himself, genuinely happy for Ardhendu. As he looked around his sweat shop, he whispered to himself, "Some other time…" before walking out of his BPO building.

⟨⟩

Ardhendu had a swanky office, a swanky laptop and a swanky phone. Behind his table was a small bar. He opened it. A bottle of Bunnahabain 18 years and a Laphroaig 10 years stood in it. A small note on the bottles said: "Welcome to RED." It was signed with a flourish: 'Colton.'

Ardhendu smiled to himself as he surveyed the room. It had been done up tastefully. Not a single thing seemed out of place. He was just about getting familiar with his new surroundings when a temp walked in.

"Hey, I am Sarita. Michelle, Mr. White's assistant had left a message for you. Your timings will be from 12 noon to midnight. She and Mr. White normally get into office by 8 pm."

"OK."

"Your laptop has been configured. Your induction process is outlined in it. You can get into WEBEXs with the US offices and you'll be up and running by tomorrow."

"Well, thank you."

"You're welcome!" she said, all professionalism, and walked out.

He did not get to see either Colton White or Michelle for the next two days.

On the third night, he met Michelle in office. What struck him about her was her extreme beauty. She stood as tall as him, an athletic, flawless physique and had deep blue eyes.

Dressed in a smart black skirt with a matching blouse, she walked up to him, a professional smile on her face, handing him a pen drive. "Colton wants you to go through the proposal for the Indian government. He wants you to meet the union minister for health next week."

"Me?"

"Yeah, you cowboy."

Ardhendu blushed and began to go through the presentation. It was about a hundred pages, with unending links to the work that RED had done in various countries, including copious details of its ground-breaking research work and drug development. A knock on his door made him look up. It was Colton White.

"Still here?"

"Um yeah, was going through this material."

"It's late."

Ardhendu looked at his watch. It was 2 am.

"Sorry, Mr. White, did not realise the time."

White smiled.

"Aren't you gonna offer me a drink?"

Ardhendu stood up, immediately.

"Sorry, yes of course, Sir."

Soon they were on the sofa, sipping their single malts.

"Ardhendu, I want you to make this presentation alone to the minister next week."

"Me, Sir? Alone?"

"Yes. You, alone."

"But Sir, I am new."

"That does not matter. At RED, we believe in empowerment and equal opportunity. So practise with me for the next few nights and we'll make sure that you do it right." There was trust and belief in White's tone.

Then, as if magically, Ardhendu began to feel different. For the first time in his life, he began to feel worthy. It seemed that this brilliant and striking giant of a man truly and completely believed in him. All of a sudden, his mother's disappointments, his teachers' covert dismissal of his abilities, his friends' ridicule of his introverted nature; all began to pale before this new-found confidence that this distinguished gentleman had bestowed on him unconditionally.

He sat up straight, his chest out for probably the first time in his life as he sucked his gut in.

"Won't you be there with me?"

"I may not be available at that point of time." The trust in White's voice was evident. "But I'll coach you to do a great job! Don't worry, all successes are yours and any failure is mine! We begin the coaching from Monday!"

✍

The following week was spent mainly behind closed doors with Colton White. White taught him all the nuances of the business, how to pitch it to the government, and what information to fall back upon, how to field questions. Finally at 4 am, one morning, White said, "That's it! You are a pro. Go home and rest. You meet the minister on Monday."

Ardhendu thanked him and began to walk away.

"By the way, here is something for you…"

Ardhendu turned around. White pulled out a small box from his desk and handed it to him.

Ardhendu opened it. A shining diamond-studded Rolex lay in it.

"The India representative of RED needs to look like one," White said in his rich baritone.

✍

Something strange happened to him. As he began to make the presentation, a passionate fire raged in him. RED was him and he was RED. The slides, the words, the figures, they all seemed superfluous! He didn't need them. His suit of midnight blue dazzled everyone. His clean narrow dark tie moved in perfect rhythm to his breathing, and probably for the first time in his life, he stood absolutely erect!

The presentation was a resounding success! The union minister went up to Ardhendu, shook his hand and told him that this would be considered and taken up in parliament. Ardhendu shook the hand firmly, holding the minister's gaze confidently. He did not feel inferior in any way to him. "We're just a few months away from the Commonwealth Games, Sir. This is just what you need. We take away the beggars from the streets, look after them, pay them, teach them a new skill and they come back as contributing citizens. In turn, we test our very safe drugs on them in an absolutely controlled environment. It's an offer sent from heaven!" Ardhendu couldn't believe he had just said that, but then he was not the self-deprecatory guy anymore.

The minister nodded his head in agreement. "We will clear this!" he said, shaking Ardhendu's hand firmly.

Ardhendu felt a tremendous sense of achievement. And he immediately called White on his mobile. The phone rang a while before he heard White at the other end.

"Er, Mr. White, I am sorry, are you unwell?"

"No, it's OK, I was sleeping."

"I am sorry, should I call you later?"

"No, no, it's OK, what happened?"

"It went well. The minister is taking it up in parliament next Monday."

"Ok, good. Great job! Look Ardhendu, let's have a drink this evening, right? Gotta let you go now."

White did sound unwell. So Ardhendu disconnected. He genuinely hoped that giant of a man would be fine. He got out into the parking to the sparkling new Hyundai the company had allocated for him. The driver opened the door and he got in. Then he drove down to the Planet M store at South Extension. It was time to celebrate. He bought the new Kishore Kumar CD and drove back home. Veena was waiting for him. Mom wasn't home and they had a good two hours alone, before she would return. Life just couldn't get any better!

By the time Mom arrived, Ardhendu was back in his suit, Veena was gone and he said bye to Mom by planting a peck on her cheek, something he hadn't done in years. Anjali looked on indulgently as he left. *"Beshi deri korishna!"* she said in that sweet melodic tone in which all Bengali mothers croon when they say goodbye to their sons.

As the car wound its way to Connaught Place, on the CD player, Kishore Kumar sang in his cheerful voice. Ardhendu saw Dharmendra serenading a beautiful Hema Malini about how he would never give up pursuing her. Delhi shone and sparkled, the bride sprucing itself up for the big day — the Games... Ardhendu smiled at the thought of a dashing Dharmendra flying a plane and singing a song for Hema Malini into his microphone...then, the absurdity of the situation made him laugh out loud. The driver looked up at the rear view mirror in surprise.

In less than ten minutes, the car arrived at the porch of the building that housed RED. He got off and acknowledged the watchman who saluted him smartly.

He walked in with the confidence of someone who had worked there all his life.

That night, White appeared pale and weak and Ardhendu observed that he needed to sit down a couple of times.

"Are you OK, Sir?"

"Ah, just a spot of Delhi belly. I'll be fine."

"Should I call the company doctor?"

"No, no," he said quickly. "I am waiting for my medicines to arrive from the US."

Almost on cue, Michelle arrived with a box.

"Colton, your medicine has just come in. Eric has brought it in."

"Eric is here?"

"Yeah, he'll be up in a minute."

White motioned to Ardhendu, "Eric Drew will head operations in India. He's from our St. Louis facility. Would you excuse me for a few moments, please?"

"Of course," said Ardhendu.

Colton White got up and walked out.

Through the glass door Ardhendu watched Eric walk into White's cabin. They emerged from there a good hour later and walked into Ardhendu's room. White introduced Eric. They shook hands warmly.

"You look much better, Mr. White."

"Oh yeah, thanks, I took my shots. They must be working right! See this piece of news?" He passed his Blackberry to Ardhendu. 'Twelve children infected with HIV by infusion of contaminated blood at a government hospital, Rampur Village, district GB Nagar,' screamed the headline of a news item. "See, now imagine if our drugs would pass muster these phases II & III of testing, we could actually save those kids. It's a crime what these governments do in terms of testing. We make life-saving drugs that can handle disasters like this, but would they let us use our drugs on them? No way, Jose! They'd rather let them die than allow us to try and save them…Why? Because our drugs haven't passed phase III & IV…human testing, that is! C'mon! Does it make any frigging sense? Does it?" White threw up his hands in mild exasperation. Ardhendu saw the truth in his statement.

"No, it doesn't." He agreed.

"Ardhendu, would you like to go to this village and ask these kids' parents if they would like to bring them to our testing centre? We could help them!"

Ardhendu gazed at the man and it dawned on him, as to how simple it actually was. "Yes, of course! I'll take care of it!" he responded, with great enthusiasm.

ᑌ

The parliament gave its clearance sooner than expected, and Ardhendu was summoned by the minister within a fortnight of submitting the proposal. The deal was on.

Ardhendu spent the next few months working with NGOs to round up poor people from dismal streets and bylanes for the rehabilitation programme.

Every day of the week was spent with the three NGOs that worked with the homeless on Delhi's streets. Ardhendu went with them to the corners of North, South and East Delhi, reaching out, talking to the poor at length, explaining the benefits of the programme. He made it a point to show them brochures of the facilities and most importantly, paid the signing amount on the spot, when any of them agreed to put a thumb impression on the documents. The lawyers of the NGOs ensured that all transactions were above board and the volunteers came of their own free will. The NGO personnel ensured that when all else failed, money was flashed to these people. Now that, worked. And how! And Ardhendu was getting closer to his goal of the first hundred volunteers.

〰

It was late evening when Michelle told him that White wanted to see him immediately. Ardhendu trotted up to his room eagerly.

"What do you think?" White asked without looking up as Ardhendu walked in.

The model of the research lab stood on the table. Built painstakingly, it was a miniature replica of the laboratory, the grounds, the living and dining areas. Little red cottages stood above ground level, surrounding a vast open field which stood on a piece of transparent glass. An underground floor was visible too. It had miniature labs, various replicas of medical machines, computers, beds and the works.

Ardhendu marvelled at the detailed structures of the rooms, with miniature beds, bathrooms and even little commodes and showers. Some of them even had Indian latrines. He couldn't help laughing out loud when he saw that.

White observed him keenly. "Hey, when you gotta go, you gotta go! Who am I to deny the way our patients would like to relieve themselves? So, comfort first!" He winked.

"What's this?" Ardhendu pointed out to a long tower jutting out from the middle of the structure.

"Oh, that's the watchtower."

Ardhendu looked up at White quizzically.

White smiled, his mouth closed.

"To keep a look out for terrorists or for that matter, religious fanatics who think we are tampering with God's creations!"

Then his face turned serious. "We have a satellite in space that monitors our logistics operations; this tower houses the communicational equipment and antennae for that. But there could be a real threat from terrorist elements; hence we want to ensure that the surrounding areas are secure. We will bring our special security forces with us to guard the place."

Ardhendu smiled back, nodding in agreement.

There was another strange structure beneath the underground building — a sort of pipe leading out of the complex. Ardhendu studied that attentively, a bit foxed.

"Oh, that's the escape tunnel."

"Escape tunnel?"

"In case we do get attacked by those nuts."

6

The first hundred volunteers were taken on board in the last week of July. Testing had already begun at the R&D lab in Uttaranchal in the remote village of Sonapani 7,000 feet up in the mountains, and Ardhendu was deputed to oversee that all was turning out well. Anjali Bose and Veena, who Ardhendu had wed in a simple ceremony a couple of months ago, had let him leave Delhi grudgingly. But work was work, and having signed up for the task, Ardhendu had no choice but to fulfil his responsibility.

Not that the task was a thankless one. In fact, far from it. Dr. Robert Schmidt, a psychiatrist on RED's rolls had flown down from the US. He had begun therapy sessions with the volunteers. Smart and empathetic American linguists on the rolls of RED conducted the communication in fluent Hindi. Ardhendu observed some of these sessions, marvelling at the detailing. Dr. Schmidt used hypnosis on the volunteers, getting them to surrender to him completely.

The Americans on RED's US team worked only US hours. Soon Ardhendu's body clock, already accustomed to his BPO days, adjusted to this new schedule.

Extensive tests were done on each volunteer. A team of highly trained doctors from the US were on standby at all times, monitoring the health of the patients: 50 males and 50 female volunteers, all from the lower strata of society. The homeless, the impoverished, the destitute who knocked the windows of your cars when you stopped at the red lights, all were here — treated with respect, fussed over constantly, and fed nutritious meals, their health monitored day and night by trained nurses. Some of them were clearly growing healthier. Soon Ardhendu looked forward to his daily rounds and small chat with the volunteers. It was magic for him as he looked at them in messianic pride. All was unfolding to format and it was time to get back to Delhi. Ardhendu was busy filing in his report when he suddenly heard someone saying: "It's all your doing, pal!"

White was at the door. Ardhendu had not realised that it was already 8 pm. He was dying to return home. He had never meant to be away so long.

"You know, we have spent a year in India today. We've made excellent progress. The home office in Kansas is very happy with all this. I am throwing a party at my penthouse tonight to thank the entire team. I'd really like you to come over."

Ardhendu looked at him in surprise. "Why, I would love to! But how on earth do we get back to Delhi from here on time? It's at least ten hours by car..."

White grinned at him. "Who says, we'll drive?"

Ardhendu looked quizzically at him. White grabbed him by the shoulder and walked him out to the exit. They took the stairs and emerged on the field above. A shining new helicopter stood there waiting.

⌒

They landed on a helipad on top of RED's building in about an hour's time. Ardhendu took the lift directly to the ground floor, got out, hurried to his company car and rushed home to change. He asked the driver to wait as he rushed up the stairs and barged in. Veena was waiting there, her face a barrage of emotions. After a quick 'Hi', he rushed into the bathroom for a shower. The warm water comforted him as it washed away the little stress and the excitement that was brimming inside him. He towelled himself vigorously and stepped out. Then he chose his best Saville Row suit out of the three that he had acquired lately, a nice grey number and began to dress. That's when Veena stepped into their room.

"Why can't I go with you?"

The expression on Veena's face made him break into a short and unexpected laugh. Veena's eyes widened. She stared disbelievingly at his reaction. This was different...he had never reacted like this...

"You're laughing at me? You don't want to take me with you anymore? What kind of a party is this?" she wailed.

"It's only for employees." Exasperated by now, Ardhendu wanted to leave as quickly as possible.

"What kind of a company is this? First, they keep you so busy that you don't have any time for me. And now they throw parties and you go alone?"

"I am a manager now. I need to be available to the organisation when they need me!"

"Well, you are not going without me!"

"Veena, please, this is not the time to throw tantrums!"

"I don't care! You are not going!"

Ardhendu had his suit on by now. Veena was standing at the door of the flat blocking the exit.

He began to advance.

"If you step out of this door now, Ardhendu, it'll be over between us."

Ardhendu looked at her, pulling her bluff. "You'll get over it in the morning. Now, please let me go..."

Veena was crying now. "You haven't even taken me to a honeymoon, yet."

"That'll happen, when it happens...now, let me go..."

"Don't you love me, anymore?"

"I do. But this has nothing to do with you...now, please, let me go."

Veena firmly stood her ground, refusing to budge.

Left with no choice, Ardhendu pushed her aside and walked out.

Veena burst into tears. She had never known Ardhendu to be so unfeeling. Ardhendu bumped into Manoj as he came up the stairs.

"Thank God you're here. She's at it again. Speak to her."

"You go ahead, I'll manage this." Manoj touched his friend on the shoulder.

"Thanks, man..."

"Shut up."

"It's over between us..." Veena wailed from above.

Anjali Bose had decided to shut herself in her bedroom.

Manoj grinned, "You go on man. This'll pass..."

"Yeah, take her out for a coffee or something..."

"Sure."

Ardhendu set out for the night.

7

Colton White's penthouse was like a seven-star hotel. Every conceivable luxury was present in it. The walls were ivory marble. Crystal and porcelain stood on the mantle pieces. Fine mahogany adorned the cabinets. French windows with darkened glass lined the entire penthouse. Expensive lamps stood in the corners. Chandeliers hung from the ceiling. The penthouse was done up completely in shades of ivory.

"Those are real diamonds," Dr. Schmidt mentioned casually. He was referring to the large chandelier that hung from the ceiling of the living room. "Champagne?" He offered a glass to Ardhendu. It was a 1968 Bollinger.

"He ain't gonna have that." Colton White came out of his bedroom holding a glass. "This is his drink." It was a Bunnahabhain, 18 years old.

"Down the hatch, buddy," Colton White egged him on.

Ardhendu did just that. Over the months, he had developed a taste; it was like liquid gold going down his throat. The crowd that had suddenly gathered around them to watch the spectacle, started to applaud.

"Friends, Romans, countrymen!" White called out aloud. "Gather please and lend me your ears!"

All of RED's thirty American employees formed a loose circle. *What a covenant!* Michelle stood in front, a red shimmering gown adorning her perfect body. Ardhendu gasped at the sight.

"I present to you our future Head of India, Operations!" Ardhendu looked expectantly at Eric, who stood there with a broad grin on his face, and wondered why Eric had not stepped forward. Suddenly he felt White's hand on his shoulder. He turned to see White grinning at him.

Then the applause broke!

It took a minute for it to dawn on Ardhendu that White was referring to him! He stood there, rooted to the spot, unable to believe this was happening. The crowd surged towards him, clapping him on the back, congratulating him, shaking his hands.

White thrust another glass in his hands. He downed it in one gulp.

"Here, keep this with you!" White thrust the black bottle in his hands. "And now, for the crowning glory of the evening! May I present, The Girls!"

A burst of thunderous music erupted from the speakers! From the drawn curtains of the dining room emerged a team of six scantily clad Indian dancers. Dressed in red, they wore matching high heels and low-necked bodices. Their toned legs gleamed in the soft light as they ran to the centre of the room flashing their perfect smiles. They cut a circle, lifted their legs rhythmically together and began the can-can. The crowd went wild! The girls then broke out and began to circle the guests, slowly pulling them into their dance. One of them caught Ardhendu and pulled him into their circle. Ardhendu allowed himself to be dragged in but stood rooted to the spot.

"Have some fun today!" White called out to him, with a wink.

"Mr. White, I have a..."

"Wife... I know! We won't tell!" He shouted merrily.

Ardhendu let loose. One of the dancers grabbed him by the waist pulling him to the floor. Ardhendu began to dance with her...

He was now six drinks old. The party was swinging and how! Someone thrust a bottle of Dom Perignon in his hands. He swigged. Michelle began to dance with White. Ardhendu, open-mouthed, watched her sensual moves.

"She's good, ain't she?" Eric nudged Ardhendu.

"Huh?"

"White's a lucky dog!"

"You mean...?"

"Oh, she'll go to the end of the world with him!"

Ardhendu set the champagne down. He grabbed a glass from the bar and poured himself a Bunnahabhain. Dr. Schmidt opened a box of Partagas Robustos. Ardhendu took one; Dr Schmidt clipped it and offered Ardhendu a light. He puffed and exhaled luxuriously...

Life was finally what he wanted it to be.

Soon the champagne and the whisky began to take their toll. Ardhendu's bladder was bursting. His head reeling, he managed to make his way to White. White turned around, a grin on his face.

"Sir, may I use your restroom please?"

White's face suddenly grew serious. "No, you gotta hold it."

Ardhendu's jaws dropped. White burst out laughing. "I'm just teasing you, man! Use the one in my bedroom, go, and spare my carpet for Pete's sake!"

Ardhendu finally got the joke. He lurched towards the bedroom.

Even in his intoxication, the sheer opulence of the room stunned him. Marble pillars, satin curtains, a king-sized bed that almost seemed to float, a thick, white rug adorning the floor; the entire room was done up in white. Heavy drapes stood over the French windows. The door to the bathroom had a gold handle. Ardhendu turned it and went inside. He reached the bowl, unzipped and let go. Ah, the relief. He would take in the opulence of the bathroom later.

Deed done, he lurched towards the basin. The tap was gold, again. He fiddled with it, wondering how it worked… Suddenly, water gushed forth miraculously. *The Great Deluge. Time for a new Ark.* He splashed copious amounts on his face. The mist cleared a bit. He took a good look at himself in the mirror. The face that looked back at him with a silly grin said, "India, Head Ops". Instinctively, he reached into his pocket, and whipped his cell phone out. Typing in Veena, he buttoned the phonebook. The number appeared. He pressed the call button.

"This number is switched off," the recorded voice told him. He shook his head and smiled. He would make it up to her. With his face still wet, he staggered out of the bathroom.

A small open bar stood above the bed with a bottle of Bunnahabhain in it. Ardhendu grinned. He walked up to it and noticed that the bottle was half full. He pulled out a nosing glass from the rack below and blew into it, then poured himself a shot, adding some Perrier. He swirled the liquid in the glass with his palm over it. Then he dove his nose in, taking two sharp sniffs. It did something to his olfactory senses. He took a sip, chewing on the liquid as though it were a solid. The complexity of the taste exploded in his mouth. He sat down on the recliner by the bed, simply enjoying the sheer luxury of it all.

He savoured the drink for a good ten minutes before finally swigging the remainder, then standing up to make his way out of the bedroom...

That's when he first heard it.

It was very faint, like the noise a howling wind makes outside a window pane on a dark stormy night. Then he heard it again. This time it was distinct. From the bedroom balcony came the muffled cry of a woman. Then all went quiet. He stood for a while. No more noises this time except for the dull thump of the music outside the door, that led to the hall. Ardhendu shook his head trying to clear it. He was probably too drunk. He began to walk out again. But this time it was clear — a woman was screaming in the balcony. Ardhendu stopped in his tracks. The crying stopped again. He turned around and strode towards the balcony. He turned the gold knob. Opening the door, he strode out.

Delhi stood out in its radiant nighttime beauty. The balcony itself was around two hundred square metres. Completely built of marble, it had pillars on which carved the statues of two semi-clad caryatides who seemed to be holding up the ceiling. A small bar stood towards the northern side. A large couch also adorned that area as did a luxurious swing. Next to the swing stood two American male employees of RED. Between them was one of the dancers. The men had her in their arms in a close embrace. One nibbled at her neck as the other watched.

Ardhendu's first reaction was to turn away from this scene. He stopped only when the woman screamed again. Shaky on his feet, he walked towards the men who had their backs to him. The woman's eyes were wide open in fear. The man who was nibbling at her neck held her in a very tight embrace. It was only then that Ardhendu noticed blood oozing out of her neck. He stiffened, shaking his head vigorously to clear it. One man had his teeth clamped firmly into the girl's neck and he seemed to be sucking her blood! Drops of the blood began to flow down her neck, on to her shoulders. The other man brought his teeth down on her left shoulder. Blood began to ooze from it.

The girl finally saw Ardhendu. In her pain, she said weakly, "Please help...me."

The two men turned around abruptly to face Ardhendu. Both doctors at the R&D lab, they stared at Ardhendu with crazed eyes. All veneer of gentility was gone from them. Their mouths were open. Their canine teeth were longer than average and their mouths were completely bloody. Blood dripped from their mouths on to their suits. A few drops splattered the floor. One of them knelt down to lick the drops off the floor.

The girl struggled to free herself, but they held her tight.

Ardhendu turned on his heels and bolted. He ran into the bedroom yelling loudly for Colton White. Then he charged towards the door leading into the living room.

Just then, White stepped in. Ardhendu ran into him full force. White did not even move an inch at the impact.

"What's up, Champ?"

"Sir, two of the men...in the balcony...that girl...they are hurting her...quick...we must stop them...please...hurry..."

"You're babbling, for Pete's sake. Calm down."

"They are attacking that girl…blood…quick… Please, please, Sir…"

"Who? Where?"

Ardhendu could only point towards the balcony.

White strode to the door, walked out, then walked back in. "Oh, that? Don't worry. They're just having some fun."

Ardhendu looked up at White stupidly.

"Really, I mean it. Listen, sit down, will you? Don't worry about that girl; she'll be better than she ever was before in a bit."

Ardhendu kept standing.

"Sit down, Ardhendu." White's voice now had the quiet tone of authority.

Ardhendu sat down on a little stool by the bed.

"Who do you think we are?" White asked as he pulled out his cigar from his coat pocket. Clipping it quickly, he lit it. "Why do you think we work only at night?" He blew out a thick cloud of smoke that created a soft haze between him and Ardhendu.

"Why do you think as an organisation we deal only with blood-related diseases? And why do you think we have come to India? Why are we really taking all these poverty-stricken people into our fold?"

Ardhendu listened in stunned silence. For the first time it struck him that he had chosen the path to perdition. Time had moved on, forever closing the door to the way back.

"No prizes for guessing…really…it's for the blood."

Ardhendu stared unblinkingly at Colton White, blood draining slowly from his face. "Blood?" he queried falteringly.

"Yes. Haven't you heard of vampires? Well, that's what we are!" White smiled now, opening his mouth for the first time. His long canines glistened in the dim light of the room.

Ardhendu stared at him in horror. For the lure of a few dollars more, Ardhendu had surrendered to the devil's brigade. The truth of the situation robbed him of all sensation in his limbs.

"You see, Ardhendu, we need human blood to survive. This world is becoming too small. Even though we are predators — and, let he who is without sin cast the first stone — it's unsafe to hunt anymore. The blood that we consume has become highly contaminated. Malaria, TB, HIV. It's no longer good for us. To survive, our species need uncontaminated blood. That's why we formed this company fifty years ago.

"Now, why have we taken all these poor people into our fold? Two reasons: to be able to complete the mass scale human testing that is required for our drugs, and to create a human blood farm where we treat them, cure them of their contamination through our drugs, and then we draw blood from them regularly for our global consumption. Makes good business sense, right?"

Ardhendu was speechless. The terror inside him intensified.

"Now, let's come to you…an operation like this needs round-the-clock supervision. We vampires cannot do that. We are allergic to the sun, dangerously allergic. So we need humans to run our operations. More so, we need a human to recruit and manage other humans who will run this organisation here in India. We have thousands of human employees in the US and Europe. We wish to replicate that model in India. You're a good kid. That's why we chose you to head our India operations! You will have everything — wealth beyond your dreams, expensive holidays abroad, a fantastic career and, most importantly, power! All you need is to be on our side, and ensure that the operations run smoothly, secretly and we get our endless supply of blood!"

White walked towards Ardhendu and put a hand on his shoulder.

"C'mon, son. It ain't as bad as it looks. You are not from a very good business school, and need this job. Why do you think we chose you?"

There was a sly grin on White's face.

"Er…this is a joke, right?" Ardhendu offered.

White stopped for a bit…then laughed.

"Come!" He said and strode towards the door that led to the living room. He opened it for Ardhendu. "Take a look."

A little relieved, Ardhendu stepped in. The first thing that struck him was that the pristine white of the living room was now no longer so. The walls, the floor and even parts of the ceiling were splattered with the colour red.

The remaining five dancers were on the floor, writhing as the band of twenty-eight Americans smothered them, biting, pulling, sucking the blood right out of their bodies. One ample-fleshed dancer had stopped twitching. Her body was covered by a band of six guests who had their teeth deep into her neck, back and arms. Three of them looked up, their mouths dripping with blood.

"How is it going, handsome?" Michelle's mouth was red, with blood-stained fingerprints on her neck, hands and dress.

Ardhendu stared at her in horror.

"Just a little celebration for the folks. Don't worry about these dancers. They were supplied by a contact who will take care of their remains!"

Ardhendu turned to White who now towered behind him. "Sir, please. Please let me go. I swear I will not tell anyone about this. Please just let me go."

"Oh dear! Are you saying that you want to quit?"

"Sir, pl...please. I cannot do this. Please, I beg you, please let me go. I will leave this town, go far away. I'll keep my mouth shut."

"Think about it. This is an opportunity you will never get in your life again. We can make your dreams come true. Vampire brigades are legion in this world. And millions are serving them for a life of luxury. Would you be different from that mob?" White spoke gently. "Listen, kid, where would you go? Most multinationals are anyway bloodsuckers. They walk into countries, exploit the resources, the people, make a packet and when they are done, they walk out...remember Exide? Or for that matter, Enron? Does that make us different? At least we're doing the real thing...we're doing something that would keep our race alive... I mean c'mon, those guys at the farm... er, lab are not being hurt..."

Ardhendu had tears in his eyes now. He was crying openly, and then he begged with folded hands. "I can't do this, please. Sir, please let me go."

White looked at him. The vampires, their gory fest halted for the time being, keenly observed the exchange.

White's forehead burrowed. A look of genuine regret crossed it. "You don't understand, I can't really let you go...believe me, this is your opportunity of a lifetime...look kid, I really like you. You're a hard-working man and this organisation needs you. Whatever you want is yours. Just name it. And don't let this cloud your soul. Look all around you. Many are doing this happily."

"Please Sir, just, please let me go…" Ardhendu was blubbering like an idiot now.

"We've come this far...you can't leave us like this now... do you know how hard it's gonna be to get someone else ready in your place?"

Ardhendu kept shaking his head from side to side, snot flowing down his nose as the tears streaked down his cheeks.

White stared at him for what seemed an eternity. Then suddenly his being filled with intense disgust at the pathetic creature that shook and shivered in front of him, sans any semblance of grace or dignity. Finally he shook his head, looked away and then fixed Ardhendu with his steely gaze.

"Right. If that's what you wish. But do shake hands with me once."

Ardhendu felt a sense of relief. In an effort to compose himself, he ran the side of his arm over his nostrils, trying to wipe the snot away. He stretched his hand out to White. White took it and shaking it firmly, said, "It was good knowing you buddy!" In a swift motion he lifted his hand, bringing Ardhendu's wrist close to his face. Then his mouth opened, and his pointed molars slashed open Ardhendu's veins.

Ardhendu watched stupidly as blood shot out from his wrist and began to drip on the floor.

"So long, Ardhendu." He turned to the rest of the vampires. "Finish him off!" Then he disappeared like a magician.

Ardhendu clutched his wrist trying to stem the flow, but the gash was deep. The vampires with bloody grins on their faces began to advance towards him. He began to back away into the bedroom, but the vampires followed. Low guttural growls emerged from their throats. Michelle led the pack, a devilish grin on her blood-smeared face.

Ardhendu looked around desperately for an escape. The only way out was the balcony, so he turned around, and opening the door, charged out. The vampires began to follow him. At the far end of the balcony, the other two, now tiring of the girl, began to move towards him. Michelle lunged at him. He flung himself back, hitting the railing of the balcony hard. The impact caused him to shift his weight. His head went over.

Ardhendu clutched at the railing, losing his hold in seconds. Then his feet slipped and his body somersaulted. It was a free fall of thirty stories.

A silent scream escaped his throat as his life flashed by him.

"Is there a catch somewhere?"

"Don't you love me, anymore?"

"It's over between us."

"You need to be self-dependent."

"Can you be happy for me, once?"

"Good Morning, Mr. Bond."

"Mom, Veena, I love you. Manoj, you will always be a friend. What was Crystal doing right now? And Mr. Gupta, the Phantom of the Indrajal comics? Where is the North Star tonight? Where? Where? Where?"

After the day's work, the crew working on the metro lines had packed enough dirt into the dumper parked just below the building on which stood the penthouse. Ardhendu fell on his back into the dirt dumper. For a while he lay there staring stupidly at the vampires who were now peering down at him from the balcony of the penthouse. "This is happening to someone else," thought Ardhendu. "I had already died the day I signed up for this job."

White looked down at him. "Three of you, quick, wash your faces and go after him. Sever his head once you are done. Make sure you kill him. Now go!"

Eric and two others dashed to the bathroom, cleaned up hurriedly, then set out on the hunt.

With superhuman effort, Ardhendu got up, realising he was still alive. Clutching his bleeding wrist, he jumped over the dumper onto the ground, and ran for his life and soul, or what remained of both.

Red, red, dread, dead…how could he just have lost his head…

"Where the hell is he?" Eric enquired on reaching the dirt dumper. Connaught Place was completely deserted at this time of the night.

"Look, drops of blood," said one of them.

"Let's go. He must be somewhere here."

Ardhendu dashed through the streets, his head reeling with shock and pain. The vampires were fast, very fast.

Ardhendu was losing blood. It gushed out from his wrist, splashing on his trousers, jacket and feet as it fell on the ground. He was weakening rapidly. Stopping behind a pillar, he tried to catch his breath.

"Think fast. How do you shake them off?"

There was no police van in sight. The nearest station was at least a kilometre away. That's when he heard Eric.

"I can smell you. Come to papa, come to papa do…!" The ghastly and eerie rendition of the song sent shivers up Ardhendu's spine.

They were very near. The vampires were fast and agile. But unlike Ardhendu, they were not familiar with their surroundings. They were not 'locals'. He knew the by lanes of Connaught Place. Terrain was his advantage as it once was for the notorious sandalwood smuggler down South. Tearing off his jacket, he tied it around his wrist, allowing it to absorb the blood. Then he slipped into the lane behind the Levi's showroom and ran as steadily as he could till he reached the liquor store on the street. Just behind it was another small lane. The entry to it was shut out by a giant iron gate. Summoning up his dwindling strength, he started to scale the gate.

"There he is!" cried out Eric.

Ardhendu reached the top and let himself drop ten feet below on the other side. He landed on his side with thud. Every bone in his body felt shattered. With great effort, he picked himself up. His left arm and shoulder felt as though they would tear out of their sockets. In his fear, he was now babbling, calling out to God, his mother, just about anyone to help him. He ran another couple of yards and then came to a dead end.

The vampires stood at the gate observing him. They flashed their canine grins.

"Here kitty, kitty…!" One of them called out.

Ardhendu fell to the ground. His head reeled. His body was giving up. He had lost several litres of blood and felt a distinct chill engulf him. Somehow, he brought himself up on his elbows and began to crawl.

The vampires were now over the gate.

That's when he felt something coarse fall on him. His body contorted in unbearable pain before losing consciousness. And the deep slumber before death sucked him into its vortex.

8

"Good morning!" He said cheerily.

Ardhendu looked up at the figure in a haze. He felt weak, very weak. His head throbbed and his body felt like he had been run over by a truck.

Slowly he took in the surroundings.

He was strapped to a bed. An intravenous needle stuck into his arm was attached to a tube that led to a small plastic bag on a stand above him. It was perhaps feeding him glucose. His wrist was heavily bandaged and his shoulder seemed to be in some sort of a plaster.

His head felt heavy and his senses somehow different. The room, more like a warehouse, smelt strongly of various things: paint, tarpaulin, various chemicals in little test tubes around him and even a half-eaten burger on the plate beside the man who leaned over him.

Ardhendu stared at him. No, Ardhendu couldn't recognise him. Around six feet tall, the man was middle-aged. Well built, he had a fairly gray beard, and hair tied in a pony tail. He wore a grey sweat shirt and a pair of Levi's jeans.

"Mr. Ardhendu Bose! Good to make your acquaintance! I am Amitava."

Ardhendu stared weakly at this man. The happenings of the night came back to him in a flash. He winced and tried to break free. "No! No! Please, let me go…" The straps were too tight and held him firmly in place. He couldn't move at all.

"Hush!" said the man. "It's OK. I am as human as they come. Don't worry. I saved you from those parasites last night." He smiled revealing two well-set rows of teeth. "See? No canines." He pointed to his molars.

Ardhendu felt a sense of relief, and then asked feebly, "Sir… where am I?"

"Oh, you are in this illegal warehouse-turned-lab of mine. You were bitten by a vampire last night and some of them almost cornered you. I followed you and whisked you away just before they could get to you."

Ardhendu looked at the man in wonder, not knowing what to believe.

"You lost a lot of blood, so I gave you a transfusion. You'll live."

"So…can I go now…please?"

"Not now. You see, you've been bitten. Unless your head is severed off, you'll turn into a vampire within twenty-four hours."

Ardhendu stiffened at this startling bit of information.

The man suddenly burst into laughter. "No, no, I am not going to do that. So relax. See this?" He pulled out a test tube with a bluish liquid. "That's twenty years of research. I finally got it right!"

Ardhendu looked at the test tube stupidly.

"Aren't you gonna ask? Go on…"

"What is it?" Ardhendu could barely manage a whisper.

"The greatest medical breakthrough in the history of mankind…the cure to vampirism!"

Ardhendu nodded weakly, only partly registering what this man was saying.

Then he observed him taking a syringe and dipping it into the test tube. Having filled it, he advanced towards Ardhendu. "This is a historic moment, my first human trial of the antivirus! This will hurt a bit and after a few minutes you will lose consciousness. But, when you come to your senses, you'll be fine!"

The man brought the syringe to Ardhendu's neck and plunged in the needle. Ardhendu screamed in agony.

The man gently took out the needle and massaged the area with his latex clad palm. "There you go. Wasn't all that bad, eh?"

Ardhendu's body was on fire. He suddenly broke out in sweat. His hair stood on end, and his skin felt like it would tear to shreds any moment. A monster with a knife seemed to carving up his insides. He screamed, his eyes rolling in his lids. His body convulsed in pain and his feet thrashed the railing of the bed rhythmically. His heart pounded loudly, threatening to tear away from his ribs and pop right out of his chest. He felt as if he would go mad with the pain.

Then the pain subsided, as suddenly as it had begun.

Ardhendu's slumped back on the bed, exhausted. Slowly he felt his head clear. A sense of peace descended on him, as though he had downed a few drinks. He felt sleepy, very sleepy. As he began to drift off, he muttered, "You said you gave me a transfusion. From where did you get the blood?"

"I gave you some of my blood! You're an O+."

Ardhendu peered at the man, "How...did you...know?"

"Of course I know! I am your father!"

Ardhendu stared hard at the man who began to fade from sight. Then he lost consciousness completely.

North Star, there you are...

9

"August '92. That's the last time I saw you. You were five then." Amitava Bose spoke warmly to his son who now sat huddled on the bed, wrapped in a rough blanket. "Still like hot chocolate? I got you some!" He handed him a warm mug.

Ardhendu accepted it gratefully. He noticed in the dimly lit room that his father's eyes, though a bit sunken with age, still had the same spark that he had remembered so well as a child.

"You see, all this goes back many years." Amitava Bose's eyes had a faraway look...

Michael Jackson did the moonwalk, his white gloves reflecting the beacons shining on him from above. His entire body moved like magic as he lip synced to 'Billie Jean'. Amitava Bose, for whom, Mithun Chakraborty jiggling his hips to Bappi Lahiri's "Taqdeer Ka Baadshah" was the ultimate dance sequence, watched in utter amazement. He became so lost in the moment that he did not hear the nurse's soft voice behind him. The big black woman's lips moved again. "Hey there, big guy!" Amitava, suddenly aware, turned his head around. "*Congratulations! It's a boy!*" She finished and waited to see the prize-winning expression on the Indian man's face.

The soft, warm light of the University of Kansas' school of medicine seemed to have taken on a comfortable glow. Amitava got up, at a loss for words. The nurse beckoned. He followed.

The baby's back fit completely on his palm. Amitava watched in silent wonder the little bundle of flesh and bones. "*My son...*" he breathed in softly. His eyes went moist. He looked around to see if anyone had noticed. Anjali smiled feebly at him. Amitava felt his chest swell up. His son in his arms, he hugged his wife.

"Tumi kandcho?" she said, indulgently, running her fingers through his hair, smoothening his brow. Amitava allowed himself to blubber with the joy he felt holding his little son as he hugged his wife. They sat like that for a while, with the nurse looking on.

She spoke with the simplicity of the Kansans, "*I like you guys, you're just as emotional as us black fools!*" She came over and put her large arms around the three, protecting them from the elements, as it were. The little family let her do so. They enjoyed the warmth silently. Anjali acknowledged the woman softly, "*Thank you, Marlissa!*"

"*Look now, what you've done...you've made me cry too!*" The big black woman responded, reproachfully.

✍

"*So what does it look like?*" Anjali asked, her baby boy snuggled comfortably in her arms, drinking his mother's milk. Her sari covered him completely. For Amitava, this was the most moving sight of all. Anjali, after three years of marriage to a man she had never known before now looked as if she had never lived without knowing him all her life.

Three days later, at home Amitava checked the chicken in the skillet. "*Here, taste this...*" He forked a piece and held it to his wife's mouth. She took a tentative nibble.

"Another five minutes." She smiled encouragingly. This was a ritual. If Amitava cooked anything, he would never switch off the burner until Anjali had confirmed that the dish was done. The curry today was made with mustard oil. He had marinated the chicken lightly with turmeric and some cloves. The seasoning was light with just one green chilli for a half kilogram of chicken. He did not want to tax his wife's stomach…she was breastfeeding, after all.

"Rice's done." He announced.

"Well?"Anjali queried, a half-smile on her pretty face.

Amitava looked intently at her. Sometimes, it seemed to him that her taana taana chokh; Maa-Durga-like eyes, overshadowed the rest of her quintessential Bengali, round visage.

"Ki holo?" she queried.

Amitava came out of his reverie. "I have a semester left, I could go into practice for a year and then apply for a H1, I guess."

Anjali looked up at her husband. No sideburns, hair worn long at the back. Tight jeans with a well fitted T-shirt, a well-toned chest and torso. The cassette player played a Kishore Kumar number; it was lullabies all the way for the little baby. She shook her head indulgently and smiled. She then looked around the little married students' apartment in the Westside of the vast campus that was the University of Kansas at Lawrence. Like her mother and many other mothers, she refused to use a diaper on the little baby. Yet, wondrously, the apartment never reflected the interesting scent from the little wet stuff that the infant produced at various intervals, of course, with little warnings to his hapless mother.

"You're a good mother!" Amitava remarked.

"Really?" Anjali blushed. "Well, I am too tired. Would you put your son to sleep?"

Amitava turned off the burner and scooped the infant in his arms. The little boy responded by cooing and snuggling comfortably into the familiar arms of his father. Amitava began to hum along with Kishore Kumar, gently rocking the baby as he slowly swayed around the room. Life to him was perfect! The $450 that he earned as a graduate assistant, paid the rent and the food, his 4.0 grade point average ensured a tuition waiver, and the love that they had for their little boy and indeed for each other compensated for whatever else they could not afford.

⌒

Dr. John English leaned forward on his desk as Amitava walked in. "Say, Amitava..." Amitava smiled inwardly at the 'Aameetaava' that came out of the Kansan's lips. "Your research project has gone well. We'd be glad to offer you an internship once your thesis is submitted." The head of the Mount Carmel group of hospitals looked proudly at this young and promising medical student who had partnered with him on a project as part of his thesis.

Amitava marvelled inwardly at the simple directness that Kansans had. His fellow countrymen would have probably built drama into that speech. The pristine white of Dr. English's office reflected the soft yellow lights on the false ceiling, giving off a cosy glow to the room. It dawned upon Amitava then that hospitals needed to look comfortable and warm, unlike the harshness of state-run hospitals back home.

"I think that would be great," he responded, using the same directness that he had picked up from the Kansans.

"Great! We'd apply for your H1 too."

⌒

"I guess then we'll soon be known as Non-Resident Indians!" Anjali remarked. Their little boy was asleep in his pram. They had a few minutes after dinner, and were enjoying the cool October breeze as they walked him by the university lake.

"Yeah…that would have made me hot in the marriage market in India, I guess," Amitava said with a half-smile, "but you wouldn't have got me…"

Anjali smiled at her husband. Amitava looked up at his wife. His studies had kept him so busy that he was glad when his father finally found a girl for him. They had met only twice, supervised by their parents in their respective homes at Calcutta. The second meeting was just a formality; Amitava had no doubt after the first one.

"Yes," he had said.

Anjali hugged him. They stood there in that embrace as the October breeze wrapped around them protectively.

⌒

"The merger was announced four years later. Rochester Edwards Corporation bought over the research arm of the Mount Carmel group of hospitals and I along with six other doctors moved over to their rolls." Ardhendu stared at his father unbelievingly. "And I became part of a team of researchers that worked exclusively on a project called 'RED Purification.' "

"What was that?"

"We studied the effects of modern medicine on human blood and worked on removing impurities from them."

"Amitava, one of the promoters is coming down to see our work tomorrow. He wants to know our progress on this." Dr. Aaron Browinski mentioned, almost in passing. "He wants to spend some time with you." Browinski's sudden nervousness did not go unnoticed by Amitava.

"Is there something specific that he needs from me?" Amitava queried softly.

"Er…he might want to know how you could speed this up."

"You can't speed up a research project like this easily..."

"Try explaining that to Colton White..." Browinski interrupted Amitava.

Amitava had had enough. It was bad enough that the culture of the organisation had completely changed ever since Rochester Edwards had taken over their wonderful research division. Their warm, friendly, yet high performance culture had somehow changed to one of high pressure and impossible deadlines. Yet, their compensation had doubled and, in some cases, trebled. Amitava's mortgage on their townhouse would now be paid off in half the time. But he still missed the old culture, the friendships, the fishing trips with his colleagues and their families, the barbecues in the backyards and the good-natured ribbing. All that had disappeared somehow.

After their very first meeting, Amitava Bose concluded that Colton White was a racist. Period. White gave him a disdainful look and came straight to the point. "Why is this taking such a long time?"

Amitava tried to maintain his calm, even though he bristled at how he was being treated. White had asked for a coffee for himself but not bothered to ask Amitava if he wanted one.

"Mr. White, a project like this takes time; it's not like I can create a magic pill that a person can take, and, presto! he becomes a pure blood or something!"

White looked Amitava up and down. "Tell me Dr. Bose, why do your people choose to come down to this country?" Amitava bristled again. White did not wait for him to finish. "It's because this country gives you the opportunity which in your country is completely denied by your red tapist, socialistic, joke of a government, right?" Again, White did not wait for him to respond, "What you'll make here in a year, you might not, in your country for in a lifetime, right?" Amitava marvelled at how this man had completely assumed that he owned him. Again, White did not wait for a response. "So, Doctor, for a change, start earning your salary! I want a full day-to-day report on what you have been doing for the past three months. And from now on, I need a daily report from you on your progress. We ain't running a charity here, get it?" White dismissed him with a wave of his hand.

Amitava walked out of his room, then straight out of the parking lot into his Toyota. He drove home.

"I'll sue the bastard!" He was on his second Scotch.

"Why do you want to waste your time on this?" Anjali asked. "After all, he did not really use any word that could be termed as racist. If you go by the book, that is."

"Yeah, he is a smart bastard. Won't use politically incorrect words…but I won't be treated like this. He made me feel like I am some sort of a mangy mongrel or something… I can't really explain…he makes me feel like I'm sub-human."

❧

"At that time, I had no idea about the significance of that statement: sub-human. But that is Colton White. Humans to him are basically sub-human!" He carried on with the story.

Amitava went back to work, but his mind was no longer in it. He decided that he was going to begin looking for another job. He was ticking off the hospitals in his mind, which was no longer on the samples in front of him. He was alone in the lab at that time of the day when Browinski tapped him on the shoulder.

"Er, Amitava…" Browinski was sweating. This was odd; after all, it was November. The Kansas skies were bright as is wont during fall, before taking on the dull gray of the winter snow.

"You Ok…?" he began to ask.

Browinski did not seem to hear. He looked around the room and then handed him a test tube. It had some blood in it. "Amitava, look, I want you to test this in secrecy, OK? And…"

Amitava looked at him quizzically as Browinski thrust it into his hands. "And, what? What's happening? You alright…?"

"And tell Jamie, that I love her." Browinski looked at Amitava for a second. Then he turned around and walked off to the corner of the lab. He opened the large French window on the wall and jumped out.

It was a windy, yet sunny Kansas morning with little white clouds floating in the air. The gardens were neatly mowed. Their verdant green formed a lovely little contrast to the lab's pristine white façade. At the foot of the Northern wall of the building ran a neat little sidewalk paved with cobble stones; very quaint and Western, a simple reminder of the state's frontier past. The six stories fall had caused Browinski's head to land squarely upon the sidewalk. Understandably, it was, smashed. His brains lay scattered around it in little white, fluffy, snowflake-like spoonfuls. His head lay at a grotesque angle against the rest of his broken body. Blood flowed from it, forming circular red pools. The colour of his blood formed a stark contrast to his spotlessly white lab coat.

Amitava took in the scene. He breathed heavily. He had run down the six stories immediately after Browinski took his leap. He watched, unmoving, his hands closing in on the test tube, hidden deep in his lab coat.

Sirens began its wails on the horizon. Something told him that the fun and games had only just begun.

Amitava was the only witness. The sheriff took his statement, shook his head and said, "I didn't know he was depressed…"

Amitava said nothing more. A few day-shift employees of the lab stood at the place shuffling their feet, talking in whispers to *each other as the ambulance bundled Browinski's body out. Colton White was unreachable on the phone.*

Amitava felt the need to be alone. His mind was a vortex. Hundreds of thoughts swirled in it. He wondered how he would break the news to his wife. Browinski's last words were, "Tell Jamie that I love her." He needed to go to Anjali too. But more than that, he wanted to test the blood sample Browinski had given him, but alone.

Colton White turned up that evening as was the norm. He held a condolence meeting where a two-minute silence was held for the departed soul. Amitava wanted to go home. It was late.

"Bose, take the rest of the day off. It's been stressful for all of us." White told him as he walked away to his office.

Bose nodded, then got up and left.

༄

Dr. Jung was the one who spoke as White entered the lab. "There is a slave who has now been without any medicine for about a year. We could try him."

"Is he here?"

"Yes."

Jung went out and brought in a man of distinct Mexican ethnicity. "He's an illegal immigrant and is willing to be a subject, provided we allow him to transform into a vampire."

White looked at the Mexican. He was about six feet tall, late twenties, clean shaven and broad chested.

"So you want to be a vampire, eh?"

"Si, Senõr." The Mexican nodded vigorously. "Give me a chance Senõr… I will not disappoint you."

White looked at him. "You know what it takes to be one of us?"

"Si, Senõr. The ability to exploit, to kill, be ruthless…"

White did not let him finish. He sprung up from his seat, grabbed the man by his neck, lifting him with one hand. Then he sank his teeth deep into his neck and began to ingest. The man was silent at first and then began squirming… White let go only when he was completely drained. He dropped the body like an unwanted newspaper. "Gracias!" he said. "It takes much more than the crap you mentioned to be one of us. It takes class." Then he turned to Jung. "Thanks. That was delicious. Get rid of him."

Jung nodded. He lifted the man's body, carried it out to the next room and placed him in a glass case in the room. He was about to hit a switch on it, when White called out to him. Jung left the room.

Amitava drove up to his home quietly by ten pm. He did it at home that night. He had refused dinner. Even his trained doctor's mind had found it difficult to eat anything after watching Browinski's brain splattered on that sidewalk.

Anjali left him alone. She knew that this man, when faced with a problem would go hide in his cave until he had sorted it out. So she let him be as he wandered off to the little lab that he had built in his garage.

Amitava did not tell her about Browinski. That could wait. He had taken a look at his little boy, who slept the sleep of the innocent in their bed. He noted dryly that unlike American mothers, his Bengali wife would not place the child in a cot. So the child slept between them…sometimes as an interruption to intimacy with his wife and most of the time as an angel that he would watch sleeping in the early hours of dawn when he himself would wake to the quietness of the morning. And his boy would *wake magically and reward him with that special smile he reserved for his father.*

He walked down quietly to his lab. Something told him that the kind of peaceful sleep that he would get with his little boy beside him, would never be his own, perhaps for the rest of his life.

What he saw through his microscope puzzled him. This was unlike any form of blood he had examined before. In fact, it was definitely not human. He picked up the phone and dialled a number. A distinctly Indian voice answered at the other end. Amitava got straight to the point. "Anand, I need your expert veterinary opinion on a particular case. Can I come and meet you, now?"

Understanding the urgency in the voice, his old friend agreed immediately. Amitava drove quietly away, with Anjali watching through the window.

"I have never seen anything like this. There is no known animal in this world that has these kinds of cells." Anand Rajaganesan's thick Tamilian accent could not hide his surprise. "This is indeed very interesting."

"What animal is it close to?"

The vet went through a thick volume on his desk. After flicking a few pages, he looked up. "It has some strains of a bat's blood, but I can't make out much more. I don't think it is of any known animal. Where did you get it from?"

Amitava thought for a moment. "Listen, Anand. Thanks. Don't worry about it. I am leaving a small sample with you. Do me a favour. If I ever ask you, just give a sample of this to the police."

"But why? What's up?"

"I cannot explain now. All I know is that there is something very wrong in this company. The way Browinski killed himself today... I am not sure if it's a safe place for me. I intend to find out what's happening...but I need you to keep this confidential."

The vet nodded. He was puzzled. But they had been friends long enough to believe each other. So he stored the blood safely in a vial.

"Oh, and Anand. You may not want to touch that blood, you never know..."

Anand put up a hand. "I'll be careful. You worry about yourself."

Amitava drove to Browinski's home. They lived far out in the countryside on a ranch. Their closest neighbour lived five miles away. It was a moonless night, one of those cold November nights, when the stars come out in all their glory, their brightness unsullied by the brilliance of a moon. In the past, on such nights, Amitava and Anjali would team up with the Browinskis, drinking Scotch while lying supine on the grass in this very ranch. They would play country music on a stereo and listen to that new singer, Garth Brooks. Sometimes, the Browinskis would leave Anjali and him alone on the grass while they fixed dinner and husband and wife would lie cheek-to-cheek counting the stars and pointing out the constellations. They were magical, those nights.

Yet this night was quite different. It felt grim, sinister and haunted.

He left his car a little up the driveway and walked the rest of the way to the house. Jamie was up. She was sitting at the porch and looked on calmly as Amitava walked up. She did not say a word. She got up, held the door open, motioning him to come in. There was no emotion on her face. She made him sit in the living room, went inside and came out with an envelope. "He said to give this to you tonight," she said, straight and simple.

Amitava took the envelope and slit it with his fingers. As he began to read, he knew that his life was about to change forever.

Amitava,

By the time you get this, I'll be dead and gone. By now you would have tested the blood and got to know that it belongs to no known human or animal on this earth. You are correct in that finding. So to get to the point, this blood belongs to Colton White. I know you will find this shocking, but you need to know this. White and his immediate team are not humans. They belong to a species popularly fictionalised as vampires. Yes, vampires. They need to consume human blood to survive. The population of vampires has dwindled through the years because modern medicine has made most human blood largely unfit for consumption for these species. Most catch infections and die in a few years. The lab is nothing but a front to help purify blood for their consumption. White himself is unwell and he has had me attending to him as his personal physician. When I told him that I can no longer be part of this, he bit me. The bite of a vampire is infectious and I will turn into one in twenty-four hours. I do not want that to happen, so I am ending my life.

White has his designs on you. He wants you to lead this research team to find an antidote that would make vampires survive on this contaminated blood as well as discover drugs that clean human blood. He will do anything to make you stay and do your assignment. So he may hold you captive, or turn you into a vampire. Either way, once you have done your job, he will exterminate you, and your family. You can essentially do nothing. These people are powerful; they will build a case against you, get you arrested, and do just about anything. Believe me, you just cannot fight against them.

I have one advice that you should heed: leave the US now. Take the first flight out, go back to India. Get your family out of here quickly. They have no presence in Asia, so you may be fine. Change your name, address, everything. Simply disappear!

There is no time. The time to act is now. I have left details of my findings on vampire physiology in a microfilm. There are some photographs that I have taken of human bodies being drained off blood. Consider these your safe passage. Jamie will give these to you. After that, she will inject herself with a drug which will act upon her in about half an hour. She will be dead too. She knows everything and has faced these guys. There is no way that she wishes to live anymore. There is no exit!

B

He looked up. Jamie handed him another envelope; this was a larger one. A trickle of blood began sneaking its way down from her nose. It began to settle down on her dry lips. She sat down and within seconds, began to convulse. Her tongue shot out of her mouth seeking air… Mercifully, she lost consciousness as the drug sped her away from this world to the next.

Amitava watched in silence. When it ended, he got up and left quietly. He ensured that no one saw him driving out, and went home. He made a phone call to his travel agent and arranged for two tickets to India. He awoke Anjali.

"But, why? I don't want to leave you here…" Anjali protested. She could not understand the urgency.

Amitava held her protectively. "Shono, trust me. I will join you in a few weeks. But you have to leave. We'll drive now. You take a flight to Chicago from where I have arranged for an Air

India flight to New Delhi. Take Ardhu and go. I need some time to wind up things. It's the best. I shall come back and begin my practice there."

"But why now?" Anjali pleaded.

"Trust me..." he held her again.

There was something in her husband's eyes that told Anjali that she should just go. He drove them to Kansas City airport, parked his car and walked them to the TWA terminal. Ardhendu slept through it all, comfortably in his father's arms. He woke briefly as Amitava transferred him to his mother.

"Bye, son," Amitava said softly to him. Sleepily he looked at his father. Amitava smiled back.

"Bye, Daddy." Then he fell asleep again. For a minute he held the two most precious gifts that he had close, his gaze capturing that moment for his mental album. Slowly, he let go of his wife and son. So they went.

Just two suitcases and her sleeping son was all she took from the country that she had once embraced to the one which would always be her own.

⌇

Colton White sat in his office. He was tired...it had been three days since Browinski had killed himself and he had spent enough time in hushing up the matter. Dr. Jung had brought him a litre of red liquid. "This is the purest we could get, Colton."

White looked at him with a mixture of disdain and anger. He grabbed it and sank his molars into it. His keen ears heard a faint click. He set it down and rushed to the window. His quick eyes spied a figure running away into the dark. "Quick!" he motioned to Dr. Jung. They opened the window and dropped down silently from it. The figure ran away into the trees. White and Jung ran soundlessly up. A trite Amitava stood beneath an oak, waiting for them. He held a camera in his hands. It had a long lens. For a second, White was taken aback. Then he understood. He motioned to Bose. "That camera. Hand it over."

"Sure," Bose said. "But let me tell you, that there are around twenty photographs of you in possession with a doctor friend of mine. They include you draining blood from a human, consuming blood from a vessel and attacking a man. All of this will go the FBI, the CIA, the Governor of Kansas, and the press, if anything happens to me."

White stopped in his tracks. He marvelled at the sheer audacity of the man. "You think anyone will believe this? We can finish you off now and no one will ever know."

"You could be right, White. But they would get suspicious once they analyse your blood sample. Browinski did not die in vain. A sample of your blood is also lying with this doctor friend of mine."

White went silent. This was serious. Discretion prevailed over valour.

"What do you want?"

"My family has reached India by now. You will lay off them. I will disappear from your life; you will never see me again. You will send two hundred thousand dollars to my wife as a patent payment. You will never look for me or try to contact my family ever again in your life and we can leave this episode behind. But if you ever try to do anything to my family, I will surface again, and it won't be nice for either of us."

White thought for a moment. "Where will you go?"

"I am not a fool. You will try to eliminate me if I tell you. So you will pronounce me dead to this world and I will find another existence. That Mexican you had for dinner the day before, I have scraped the skin off his fingers and pasted my skin on them. The prints are mine." Amitava raised his right palm. He had bandages on his fingers. "Tell the world it was me."

"And if I refuse?"

"You really don't have a choice."

White could not help but admire Amitava's resourcefulness. He smiled suddenly. "Brilliant! I knew you had it in you. Listen, Doc. I need you. You are the best researcher I have. The vitamins developed by Browinski work for my species, but ultimately, we need pure blood to consume. You can create those drugs for us. Continue working for us and you'll see wealth beyond your imagination. Your family will be safe...you will..."

"End up like Browinski someday? I think not..."

White looked at him, his temper rising, "Why, you two bit piece of brown shit... I'll tear you apart with my bare hands..."

"I don't exist anymore, White." Amitava said matter-of-factly. "I died in that lab fire."

"What? Which fire are you talking about?"

"That one..." Amitava pointed ahead.

Colton White turned around. Fumes of fine smoke wafted out of the lab's windows. Their fine grey and acrid smell blended in with the pure Kansan night air. White jumped. He turned around, "You little piece of..."

He was talking to thin air. The explosion occurred then, taking the roof of the lab with it.

"The only reason White hired you son, was to see if he could get his hands on me. Everything he does is pre-planned. I am a qualified doctor. White had me working on various vaccines for blood-related diseases. So, one day, I followed his car to his home where I found him consuming it. After that, I kept tabs on the rest of the gang and discovered what they really were.

I first thought this was some sick cult, but then soon realised that everything that Browinski had written about was true. However, at RED you can check out anytime you like, but you can never...you know the rest.

"Soon after that, I set my lab on fire, and faked my own death. I actually killed one of the human slaves they employ."

Ardhendu looked at his father quizzically. "Human slaves?"

"Oh, yeah. These bloodsuckers keep many human slaves, really sick losers that willingly give their blood away to vampires for money and the promise that they will be turned into vampires some day. White drained one of these guys one day and he was kept in a glass case until he turned into a vampire.

"So I killed this joker, scraped away the skin on his fingers and replaced them with mine. Then I placed his body in the lab which I set on fire. The authorities thought that I had died in that fire. After that I boarded a ship back to India, one of those that carry illegal immigrants, created a new identity and ever since, have lived anonymously in this warehouse trying to find a cure to vampirism."

"Why did you not contact us all these years?" Something in Ardhendu stirred.

"And put you guys in danger? Had I surfaced in India after all my records showed that I was dead, it would have made the press. After which these bloodsuckers would have traced me down and eliminated you, your mother and perhaps my entire family tree."

There was silence.

Amitava Bose walked up to his son. He put his arm on his shoulder. "I missed you son as I missed your mother. I have led a lonely life here. I have walked by you so many times; I have silently seen you grow up from afar. It...it hasn't been easy."

Both father and son fought back their tears. Then suddenly, the ties of blood washed away the distance and pain as Ardhendu reached out and hugged his father.

"I still cannot be seen with you, son. This is not over yet. You need to go quickly and fetch your mother. Leave town tonight. Take the train, not an airplane. They can blow up a plane, but will think twice before they try anything in a train. Go to Calcutta and drive to my ancestral village in Sreerampur. Your mother would have told you that my late Maternal Grand Uncle has a farm there." Ardhendu nodded, recollecting weakly. "His people will expect you there and they will take care of you. Do not step out of the village until you hear from me. And no, they won't be able to get you there. They have three hundred acres of land in the village. My Grand Uncle had no family. His caretaker is the only one who knows I am alive. And the only crop they grow is garlic. These parasites would not survive within a radius of fifty miles!"

✑

"But why Calcutta?"

"Mom, just get onto the train, and I'll explain!"

The crowd on the platform almost engulfed the train which was about to leave.

"Really, Ardhendu, what's this about?"

"Mom, please. Trust me."

He sat his mother in the 2nd AC compartment and quickly shoved their bags under the lower berths.

"We have around fifteen minutes. Let me get some water."

He stepped out on the platform. The sea of humanity overwhelmed him as he made his way to the snack stall. He bought two bottles of water. He opened one and began to drink from it. Soon he had finished the entire bottle. He began to head back to the train. That's when he felt the thirst again. He realised that he hadn't had any water since the night before. He opened the other bottle, put it to his lips, and headed back to the stall to get some more bottles. He realised he had drained the second bottle as well. His throat felt parched now. There was a tap nearby. He ran across to it, and opening it, he began to gulp voraciously. Then slowly, he made his way back to the AC compartment and sat by his mother. An odd chill began to pervade his bones. The smells around him grew stronger. His eyes began to open wide and he looked around. A sense of unease crept over him. Suddenly he became hyperactive. He looked at the people around him in distaste. He was thirsty. He wondered why, since by then he must have had at least three litres of water in him.

"Ouch!" winced Anjali Bose. She had pricked her little finger on the safety pin which she had taken out from her sari. A tiny drop of blood appeared on it. Ardhendu could not take his eyes off that drop. All of a sudden, the animal in him seemed to take control. His mind swerved. He stared at the finger, he wanted to grab it, he wanted to bring it to his mouth, he wanted to sink his teeth into it, draw all the blood out, into him. He wanted to feel that blood on his tongue, his lips, his teeth. The smell of the blood, warm, heavy, intoxicating, began to overwhelm him. He brought his face closer.

"What are you doing?" Anjali barked at her son.

That brought him out of his reverie. He stared at his mother. For a minute, the world came to standstill. Then it dawned.

"We have to get off. Right away, Mom."

"What?"

"There is no time, Mom, we have to get off!"

"Ardhu, what's the matter with you?"

He grabbed his mother's arm, and started walking away from their seats. He managed to pull her out of the bogey just as the guard blew the whistle.

⟁

"He was drunk and insisted on dropping the dancers off. Since he was the only local in the party, we allowed him to. He disappeared after that and there's no trace of the girls either."

Ramesh Tyagi had a very sombre face.

The commissioner of police, TK Paul looked on pensively. "We sent a team to his flat. It's locked. His mother has not reported to work either."

"Sir, this will look really bad on the international arena. After all, this is the first major multinational Life Sciences investment in India in the past two years. This is also bad for Indo-American relations."

"I know, I know," the commissioner sighed.

"The American Ambassador has been here once, the press is on my head and the Indo-American Chamber of Commerce wants a statement. Listen, tell Mr. White and his colleagues that we will provide them with twenty-four hours security cover."

"Is that enough…?"

"We'll get that Ardhendu Bose." The commissioner cut Tyagi short.

Tyagi shook hands and walked out. He pulled out his mobile and dialled a number. White picked up at the other end. He was in his bed. It was as dark as night in there. The heavy drapes shut out all sunlight. He heard Tyagi out. "For a human, you do have your moments, Tyagi!"

Tyagi's excited voice could be heard over the speaker. "Why, thank you Mr. White! Thank you!"

White disconnected the phone. He turned to his side. Michelle opened the door to his room. "There's anything you need, Colton..."

White snarled at her like a rabid wolf, "Shut that goddamn door, woman! You're letting the light in!"

10

"I gave you a high-end cocktail of haemopoietic drugs. That's supposed to stimulate your existing bone marrow to produce red blood cells. A much weaker version is used for leukemia patients. It worked in your case, but only for twenty-four hours." Amitava Bose observed thoughtfully. "The infection from the vampire bite is too strong. It destroys bone marrow production completely; that's why the need for them to consume blood. I have been developing this cocktail for the past twenty years, but obviously, it's not strong enough."

Ardhendu was strapped to the bed. Anjali Bose had lost her voice. She was in deep shock, first at seeing her 'dead' husband alive after twenty years and next at trying to fathom what had happened to her son. She sat like a statue with her mouth open, mutely observing the goings-on.

Amitava Bose did his thing with the syringe. Ardhendu went into convulsions, then lost consciousness.

Amitava went up to his wife. He put his hand under her chin. "You still look beautiful…"

Her eyes which were moist now, began to blaze. "How could you?" she thundered. "How could you lie to me like this? How could you leave us alone like this? How could you…" Then love overpowered her as she put her arms around him and broke down. The only man she had ever loved was finally back with her. Something terrible had happened to her son. She didn't exactly understand what, but now that her man was back, she believed that he would take care of things.

Amitava held her close, his silence offering comfort to the woman who had led the life of a widow for two decades, raising a boy on her own. He was not going to interrupt what she would have to say.

And she had a lot to say. She spoke the whole night as her son slept.

⌇

"What has happened to me?" Ardhendu cried. He had regained consciousness some ten minutes ago.

"Son, you will need to be strong. What has happened to you is unfortunate."

"Dad, please save me from this!"

"Look son, there is no point in hiding this from you…you have to listen carefully. After being bitten by Colton White, you would have died from blood loss. I saved you by transfusing some of my blood to you. I also gave you this injection which stimulates bone marrow production. Because of this, you won't get the vampiric blood thirst. However, I realise that the haemopoietic drug cocktail seems to be effective for only twenty-four hours. So you will need to take this every day. We do not have a choice for now."

"But, Dad, what have I become?"

"Son, you are now a vampire."

Ardhendu looked at his father in utter horror.

"This can't be, I have to go…" he began to tear away at the straps.

"Where are you going?"

"I have to meet Veena, explain to her, we can run away."

"You cannot do any such thing?"

"Why not?" Ardhendu screamed.

"Because you may end up infecting her!"

There was stunned silence in the room.

"Your saliva, blood, semen, all of this can end up infecting a human being. You'll need to live life now in a sterile manner. Wear gloves, ensure that you do not touch unnecessarily. You should keep your nails real short. A scratch from you might end up infecting a human if it is deep enough. You see, most vampires keep their nails very short, if not actually remove them completely. I'll have to do regular tests on you. I'm sorry son, but you cannot have any physical relations with human beings from now on. Even your mother should avoid getting too close to you!"

Ardhendu ran to the little window on the wall. It had three iron grills. He held onto them and broke down. "Dad, please don't tell me all this. I just wanted an ordinary life. I cannot go through all this. Please, Dad," he cried as his body convulsed with his sobs.

"Why don't you give me one of your medicines that will just kill me off, Dad? I cannot go through life like this. What have I done to deserve this?" Ardhendu sobbed uncontrollably.

His mother ran towards him, her arms outstretched, only to be stopped by his father.

When the sobbing subsided, Amitava said, "Take a look at the grills, son."

Ardhendu looked up. The iron grills in his hands were now bent out of shape. He let go immediately, staring at them in despair.

"Yes. You did that."

Ardhendu turned around. He stared at his hands in horror.

"You have the vampire's strengths and also all their weaknesses. I have however developed some drugs that are helping you."

Ardhendu saw a faint ray of hope. "Really? What...what are they?"

"No, they won't cure you, but they will help you. See, in my research for a cure to vampirism, I have studied and experimented heavily. Today I know all there is to know about vampires and their bodily systems. Based on that, I have created a combination of very strong cortico-steroids. These are very strong anti-allergic medicines. They have protected you from the sun, silver and garlic. The sun will make you feel very hot; you may break out in rashes but it won't burn you, you won't combust. Garlic and silver may give you rashes and an itch, but won't kill you. Again, going by what I saw and how long these would last, you would need these shots every day. So think about it..."

"What?" Ardhendu asked.

"I have been fighting this war alone against these bloodsuckers for two decades. I need some help. Why don't you join me in this fight?"

"Amitava, no..." Anjali protested.

"Shh. Think about it, son. Everything happens for a reason. There is a reason why this happened to you. Think about it. You have their strengths and my medicine will keep you from their weaknesses. Look at what they have done to you. Think about what they are trying to do to those poor people of our country. They feel that we in India are a third world people so they feel they can make human poultry farms out of us with complete impunity!

"You are the only person in this whole wide world who has the strength and probably the intelligence to battle them. I know everything about vampires, their bodies, the way they think, and the way they operate. I will teach you. Come, son, join me. Let's finish these parasites off once and for all."

Ardhendu was quiet for a while. When he spoke, his voice was choked with emotion. "I haven't fought a single fight in my entire life. I have never been aggressive. Why, I was even a failure at sports. I am frightened of these creatures, Dad. Maybe you should just kill me, Dad. I don't want to live anymore, please Dad, please give me one of your injections and kill me…please…"

Amitava could not stand the sight of what his son had turned out to be. He turned to his wife. "Is this what you've done to my son? Raised him to be a sissy? What have you done? Dominated him all his life, made him feel small, so that you could control him all your life? Or is it that he never met your high standards?"

Anjali, looked up in shock at her husband as the reality of his words sunk in. "I… I only wanted him to be like you…" she trailed off, her mind trying to brush away the impact of the ugly truth.

"Make him like me? Like me? I wouldn't want him to go through what I went through in a hundred years…living the life of a fugitive, not knowing when I would be caught, not being able to hold my own son to my chest…you wanted him to be like me? Has it ever occurred to you that it was more important for him to be like him? Get this, Anjali, no father would ever want his son to go through what he has." He paused as he watched his son cry like a baby. "You must be proud, real proud!" He said to his wife. Then he turned to his son. "You want to die? Take the easy way out? No son of mine is going to be a sissy. You will fight! I have fought. We all have to fight a fight in life. It is just that your fight is different! But it's a fight alright!"

"Dad, I can't fight!"Ardhendu blubbered.

"Yes, you can! Bloody hell! This is your war! YOUR WAR AGAINST THESE PARASITES WHO DARE TO THINK THAT THEY CAN SUBDUE HUMANS! YOUR FIGHT AGAINST WHITE WHO HAS TURNED ME INTO A FUGITIVE AND MY SON INTO A MONSTER! Are you going to let them be for what they did to you? Your love life is finished. YOU can never be human again. YOU can never be normal again. So are you going to let them go for that? Are you going to turn your other cheek, ARE YOU?" Amitava roared.

Ardhendu clutched his head...his father's words stung him like a swarm of bees. He cupped his ears, covering them, trying to block out those words, but they stayed, ringing loud and clear. Suddenly, a new emotion dawned inside him...it was anger. Anger at what had become of him, anger at how he had been treated by this world, anger at how all this had turned out...

From deep down his throat rose a guttural growl. It culminated into an animal roar. With his right hand he lifted the king-sized bed cleanly above his head and brought it down to the floor. The bed splintered to pieces. Then he jumped back, staring in fear at what he had just done.

Anjali Bose watched in amazement, shock and horror. Ardhendu stared at the broken bed, too shocked to speak. He did not know what had hit him...and began to back off.

"I... I can't do this, please, I have to go. Please..."

Suddenly things began to appear hazy; the loss of blood, the events and the shock took their toll. His father's visage began to shimmer, the warehouse began to spin, and then the ground came up to meet him. He fell hard on his face, losing consciousness, again.

Anjali Bose ran to her son. She was crying loudly now. She tried to hold her son as Amitava looked on calmly. "I'll take care of him," he said quietly as he knelt down and lifted his son's unconscious body in his arms. He put him on the couch and took out a syringe...

⌁

Ardhendu regained consciousness the next night. He had slept for twenty hours. There was no one in the warehouse at that time. His parents were either upstairs or outside. He couldn't see or hear them. He realised that he was no longer strapped to the bed. So he threw off the covers and broke into a run. He ran quickly on the streets of Delhi. He felt lighter, stronger and had developed an inordinate sense of smell and vision. He ran for two hours until he reached the building where he had stayed with his mother and Veena.

He went behind the building. In a single leap, he scaled the wall. He clung to the pipe and began to climb it till he reached the fourth floor.

Veena slept in fits and starts. When she heard the knock on the window, she went to it and opened it.

Ardhendu jumped lithely into the room.

She stared at him disbelievingly.

"Veena, honey, it's so good to see you. Oh, I missed you so much."

Veena stood in shock.

"You'll never believe what happened to me, I'll explain on the way...come quick, pack your stuff, we're leaving."

Veena did not budge.

"Come, on, we don't have time. Let's go down the pipe. Quick, we are leaving town. Come now, there's no time to lose."

Veena did not move an inch.

"Come on now," Ardhendu reached for her.

She shrank back in horror.

"Ardhendu, the police are looking for you," she whispered.

"I know, that's why I am saying, let's go."

"I am not going anywhere with you."

"What?"

"You have committed a crime. The police said that you were drunk, on drugs and that you kidnapped five girls and disappeared with them. They said that you also assaulted the RED employees. They've talked to me twice and had called me to the station."

"Veena, that's a lie. I have been framed. You don't know what really happened! It's something else. They're not who we think they are. Listen, I can explain, but right now, we need to leave town. So come, let's go."

"The only person who is going is you."

Ardhendu stared unbelievingly at the woman he loved.

She turned away from him, "I cannot stay married to a man who is a fugitive. You have screwed up your career... It's over between us."

"No! It's not true, believe me..."

"The police have posted two constables here. If you don't leave now, I'll have to call them."

"Veena, no, sweetheart, don't do this to me...listen, I love you, and you are the only one I have in this world..."

"Don't come nearer, or else I'll scream."

"No, sweetheart, please..."

"Watchman!" Veena's shrill scream cut through the silence of the night like a knife.

Ardhendu froze. He watched without moving as the steps outside the door grew louder, as someone began to pound on the door, as Veena opened the door screaming and shouting, "He's here! Oh please, save me from him!"

He saw the woman he loved run out of the door and hide behind the two constables and four guards who burst into the room. He watched as the constables raised their rifles at him, commanding him to put his hands up, as they repeated the command, as they cocked their hammers, ready to pull the triggers.

He watched without moving as his simple life disappeared from his eyes completely. The sadness inside him began to boil; it simmered until it overpowered him. Then it turned into something else...

He watched as one of the constables said to the other, "Fire at the count of three...

"One, two..."

His upper lip lifted, baring his canines. His blue eyes pierced those of the constables. Then he trained his sight on the guards with their *lathis*. A low growl turned into a full-throated snarl. The constables' reaction was quick. They dropped their rifles and ran. The guards followed suit.

106

Only Veena was left standing there. He stared at her, his eyes burning into hers. She put a hand on her mouth and screamed! This time, in genuine fear.

He turned and jumped out of the window.

11

"Vampirism is a disease." Amitava Bose's tone was informational, almost educational. He punched a few keys on his laptop. An image floated on the screen. It was that of a man, with his innards visible.

"Around the 12th century, some vampire bats in Romania developed a peculiar form of rabies. The strains of this virus caused these bats to behave in an extremely aggressive manner. Instead of feeding quietly on cows or goats, they began to attack predators. A few of these mated and infected other bats in the castle of a man well known by folklore. He was Prince Vlad."

Ardhendu looked at his father, "Wasn't this the same person on whom Bram Stoker had based his Dracula?"

"Exactly. Legend normally has its roots in fact. I have done enough research to be able to point out fairly accurately that Vlad did indeed get bitten by these bats.

"Once in contact with a human, the strain mutated to abnormal forms. Rabid humans develop a fear of water.

This mutated strain did something else. It caused a very severe skin condition, aggravating what Vlad already was. He was sensitive to the sun. The strain caused his skin to burn when in contact with the sun. Slowly it would cause sores and when fully developed, instant combustion. The other effects would be extreme allergy to certain elements. Humans are fatally allergic to mercury. Vlad became severely allergic to silver. A cut by anything in silver can cause instant gangrene for vampires. This virus also made him severely allergic to garlic. Consumed in any form, garlic can cause the swelling of the food pipe of a vampire, enlarging it with severe internal boils. This would further cause choking in the individual, leading to a horrific death. Also garlic, if sprayed into the eyes of a vampire, can cause instant and permanent blindness."

Ardhendu listened attentively.

"Here is what happens when bitten by those rabid vampire bats."

The image on the screen showed an animated bat biting the human form on the neck. The strain of the bite then entered the blood stream causing enormous bubbles. The jugular vein began to open, forming a vein that moved up to the canine teeth.

"This is interesting. Within twenty-four hours of being bitten by a vampire, the jugular vein develops a canal to the canine teeth. The tooth develops a root."

Amitava used the mouse to zero in on the image of the tooth on his laptop.

"The teeth become sharper, gaining in length, but not to the absurd lengths shown in films. Vampires look as threatening or as harmless as any other human. This allows the teeth to suck the blood and deposit it directly to the jugular vein, thus filling the veins with the host's blood."

"Does it mean that they do not need normal food?" Ardhendu queried.

"No, they do. They develop extremely high metabolism, so they need to feed constantly. They need a high-protein diet, so meat is essential for them. They are carnivores. Their problem is that the strain directly attacks their bone marrow causing it to cease production. So…"

"…they need to consume human blood to be able to survive." Ardhendu finished his father's sentence.

"Yes. They do."

"But, humans have different blood groups, so how can they drink blood and…"

"Correction! Vampires do not drink blood; they use their canine teeth to inject blood directly into their jugular veins. The strain causes their blood groups to mutate. Their bodies become receptive to all groups, and mix them together to form their lifeline."

Ardhendu listened in fascination. "Like a good blended scotch whisky."

Amitava smiled. "The mutation causes something else: extreme levels of testosterone; this generates extreme aggression in them. The taste and smell of blood also increases this testosterone, making them very animal-like when they hunt. In fact, some of their altered DNA has a curious mix of the bat and the wolf. Why? I don't know.

"The virus also selectively targets the anabolic steroid producing cells and stimulates them, acting just like normal steroids. It causes these cells to multiply, thereby causing vampires to become four times stronger than normal humans. All cells in the body then begin to regenerate four times faster than normal human beings. This then…"

"...causes their life span to become four times that of a normal human."

This time the older Bose simply grinned at his son's quick grasp of Science.

"So, you see, Vlad spawned a new species. On discovering his new strengths and flaws, he impregnated his wife; a child was born to them, who was the first pure vampire. Vlad's exploits include cutting off the heads of his opponents and impaling them on sticks. He did this for a specific reason; vampirism is infectious, just like HIV. The only way you can stop an infected human from turning into one, is to severe the head so that the brain cannot control the body. Vlad learned that soon enough. He burned down the forest that housed these bats and then carefully spawned a small group of vampires, including siring one. This group grew in size. Soon continental Europe, on becoming aware, began to hunt them in daylight, causing their numbers to shrink. That's when these vampires began to hide their presence from the world. They operated in secret. By the 18th century, they formed their own unions, always operating silently, without letting their presence known. Soon, truth became legend. By the 20th century, many medicines were let loose on the market. These caused human blood to become contaminated. New diseases, hitherto unheard of, held sway. On consuming this blood, vampires fell sick. Some began to perish. That is when some well-to-do vampires got together to build this company in the 1900s. Their aim was to create medicines that would de-contaminate human blood, to create a survival mechanism for their species."

"Understandable," said Ardhendu.

"Yes. Nothing wrong with that. A lot of blood banks in Europe and the US are actually owned by vampires. In my opinion, that was OK. At least, it was not necessary for them to attack humans."

"Then what is wrong with Colton White and his band of merry bloodsuckers?"

"Colton White hails from a family of great wealth. He was born a vampire. He actually formed this company. He has been alive for almost two centuries now, emigrating from Europe to the Americas so that Europeans would not suspect his non-ageing. His vision is different from other vampires."

"What is it?" Ardhendu queried.

"White views us humans as cattle, no, actually much lower in the evolution scale: poultry to be more precise. He has no respect for us as a species. He looks at us only as a source of food and pure profit. His ultimate aim is total dominance of humans. He wishes to turn this world into one large human farm. His ideas of human testing centres never got much buy in the Western world, so his strategy works well in our country. Millions of people below the poverty line; a multinational company with deep pockets, willing to take on the embarrassment of this country as their 'moral' responsibility. A corrupt health minister who takes money to allow phase III and IV human trails without proper government supervision… It's a godsend for him…you get the drift?"

Ardhendu looked up. Visions of the health minister floated in his mind. "You mean that…"

"RED lined his pockets long before they even came to India. He has a neat pile now in a nice bank in Zurich." Amitava shattered the illusion.

Ardhendu stared at this man whom he had never known for most of his conscious life. Yet, he felt inexplicably drawn to him; perhaps blood was thicker than water.

"You have understood what makes vampires. You now need to understand how to combat them."

Ardhendu stood quietly.

"I have explained your uniqueness. This is caused by the antivirus. However, there is a way to enhance your strength, agility and speed."

"How?"

"With steroids."

Ardhendu looked up.

"Steroids injected into you will simply affect your already enhanced anabolic cells, causing them to multiply and increase your strength to at least three to four times of that of an average vampire..."

"...making me a perfect vampire killing machine..."

"Let me put it this way...you'll give Buffy a complex."

The humour was lost on Ardhendu.

⟿

The next day Ardhendu and his father were up early.

"You need to learn a martial art. Here are some DVDs. Watch them carefully and practise."

Ardhendu began his practice under his father's observant eyes. His new-found strength and agility made him pick up moves very quickly. Amitava Bose began a strict regimen with his son. They practised for twelve hours every day. In between, Amitava Bose would inject him with steroids, constantly monitoring his blood pressure and lipid profile levels.

Anjali Bose joined him at the sessions as Ardhendu lifted a six hundred pound bench press.

"You're working hard on him."

"Yes, I am making the perfect killing machine."

Anjali Bose watched her son sadly, horrified at her husband's statement. "How do you do it?" she asked.

"Do what?"

"Stay stoic and calm over such a horrible tragedy?"

"What did you call it?"

"A horrible tragedy…you working for this company twenty years ago, discovering their secret, sending us away, living in hiding all these years, and then of all companies, your son gets a job here…how can you still remain calm and strong and not break down?"

Amitava looked at his wife, as his son, replacing the barbells, sat on the bench press, observing the exchange silently.

"Who called it a horrible tragedy?" he asked his wife.

"Well, it is a horrible tragedy, it is a…"

"Who called it one?" he asked again, gently.

Anjali finally heard the question. She thought for a while, and said, "Isn't it a horrible tragedy?"

"Who called it that?" Amitava repeated the question…

"I did," Anjali admitted.

"Yes, you did. It wasn't me. The way I look at it, this has happened and that's it. I haven't given it an adjective, haven't described it. In short, I haven't made things significant. For, once I start calling it a horrible tragedy, it starts becoming one for me. And when it does, my description of it will cause me to weaken. The issue is that that's what we humans do. Make everything significant. Once you stop doing that, it becomes much easier to deal with events that take place in our lives."

Anjali heard him out and those words began to sting her. She realised that all her life, this is exactly what she had done, made things significant.

"So, what should I do?" She asked her husband.

"Stop making things significant. Your husband is living incognito and your son is a vampire. That's it. There is no meaning in it. Just accept that and stop thinking about it. You will get into action. And that is precisely what we need from you. We are a family again and we have each other and that's all that we need."

Amitava gently touched Anjali's cheek. She looked around at Ardhendu longingly, her eyes beseeching him to come and join them in a family embrace, but the creature that sat on the bench, felt no emotion for this woman he had once called Mom. The only love that he had in him was for his father and he felt no desire to share it with anybody. Not in this lifetime at least. He looked at them and decided not to interrupt their moment of intimacy. Then he turned away and walked out.

Amitava let him leave. He didn't say a word. He didn't make things significant.

✍

Thirty days later Amitava Bose approached Ardhendu with a couple of two foot-long switchblades.

"These are made of silver. The shape allows for hacking, chopping and other moves. Each blow from these can be fatal for a vampire. You now need to learn how to use these."

Ardhendu swung the blades.

Amitava looked at him without expression. The warehouse was Spartan. He placed two candles on the table.

"Slice them," he said simply.

Ardhendu swung the blades again. "What about bullets? Don't they affect them?"

"It's a strange thing…bullets wound them…but their bodies tend to reject the bullets a few hours after they are shot. So even when you shoot a vampire, it will still come at you, thanks to its testosterone."

It was late at night. They stood on top of the Levi's showroom at Connaught Place. The thirty-story tower on which stood RED's India office gleamed in the moonlight.

"You have inherited the vampire's agility. Now you need to develop that. Have you heard of Parkour?"

"It's a French sport, something that has to do with obstacles in one's surroundings."

"Yes. Well your obstacles are these buildings. You need to be able to jump, run, leap across all these buildings in Connaught Place. You need to become as familiar with them as you are with the back of your hand. Every lamp post needs to be your swing, every window your diving board. Your familiarity with this place will be your weapon against the vampires.

"Now I am going to time you. Jump down from this building, climb the next; you need to cover each building in the inner circle in less than thirty minutes. Now go!"

Ardhendu leaped.

12

Ameeta was dancing wildly. It was the concoction of rum, vodka and marijuana. The techno beat in the nightclub had her and the other PYT in a clingy top and jeans in a frenzy.

The tall and handsome American with her shouted into her ear. "Want to have some more fun?"

"What?" she screamed.

"Some more fun?"

"Sure!"

"Let's show you some heights!"

For a girl working at a call centre, the attention of these two good-looking and understandably, loaded, white American men was very flattering. They had come this Saturday night to this happening nightclub, since ladies always got a free entry. The beer was what they could afford; otherwise it was pretty easy to make eyes at some bloke at the bar who would willingly shell out for drinks just for the company of these girls. Many considered it a privilege. So it was just befitting that these two sophisticated white men had approached them very gallantly, inviting the PYTs to join them at the exclusive and more expensive area of the nightclub. The men had ordered fine French champagne in a bucket. This was the night for Ameeta and her petite friend, so they immediately accepted the offer to go somewhere even more exclusive.

After the drinks, they went up to the terrace of the 5-star hotel in Bhikaji Kama Place. Delhi by night was beautiful!

"So what's the fun?"

"This, baby!"

One of the men grabbed Ameeta's friend and began to nibble at her neck. She giggled.

"Like that?"

"Ooh," she cooed.

"Then you're gonna love this…"

The man opened his mouth wide, his canines glistening in the moonlight as he brought them down on the nape of her neck holding her in an unmovable lock.

The girl screamed.

Ameeta watched, her intoxication dissolving…

Blood flowed from the girl's neck. The other American jumped down on her and began to lick the flow. The man who had his teeth locked on her neck, removed himself, then raising his eyes to the moon, opened his bloody mouth wide and growled.

The other man now brought his canines down on the other side of her neck.

Ameeta screamed. The two men fell upon the girls like animals.

Ameeta began to run. She crossed the terrace and ran towards the gate that would lead her downstairs. Her date stood in her way.

"Oh, please don't leave. The party's just begun," he hissed, his mouth bloody, with drops splashing over his jacket.

Ameeta watched in horror as the man slapped her across the face. The sheer force of the slap made her whirl and drop to the floor of the terrace. She was speechless as he stood in front of her, his bloody face contorted in a hideous grin. She put her hand on her mouth, tears streaming from her eyes. "Oh God! Please, let me go…"

"God?" he said. "Where?!"

"Nowhere."

The man turned around.

At the door stood a figure in a black leather jacket and black leather jeans. His hair was short, almost in a crew cut. His face, expressionless. When he spoke, it seemed only his lips moved. His voice came out in a low throaty growl. "Just the devil!"

Dr. Robert Schmidt's bloodlust had gotten the better of him. All his carefully crafted veneer of gentility was lost now in his predatory frenzy. The blood was fresh, it's taste intoxicating. He stared at this intruder. His sudden anger at the interruption now metamorphosed into the anticipation of another kill. With a scream he rushed towards the intruder.

Ardhendu did not move until the vampire was at arm's length. He raised his right foot and kicked him in the solar plexus.

Dr. Schmidt watched helplessly as the kick took two of his ribs, flinging him with massive force back onto the terrace.

Hearing the commotion, the other vampire joined him. He glared angrily at the sight. Then he took a leap and landed in front of the intruder. "You dare?" he roared. He swung his hand in front of him, his nails tearing away at Ardhendu's leather jacket.

Ardhendu caught his hand, and turning him around mid-air, made him land heavily on his back.

The vampires, not used to being attacked, lay on the terrace for a few seconds in shock. Ardhendu stood close to them, his face expressionless.

The two got up. Like cheetahs, they circled him. Ardhendu did not move. His eyes followed their movements.

"In hand-to-hand combat with vampires, always let them make their first move. Over the centuries, they have forgotten the art of combat. So confident are they of their strength, they simply use their nails and teeth to attack." Amitava Bose's advice stayed in Ardhendu's mind.

The two leaped at Ardhendu. In a flash, Ardhendu used his hands in sweeping motions. He landed a chop on Dr. Schmidt's collar bone, breaking it into two, and used his left elbow to land a blow at the other's chin. A bloody geyser erupted from the vampire's mouth.

The two, now injured, stared in stunned surprise at this creature.

Dr. Schmidt broke into a rage again. "We will tear you apart limb by limb!"

Ardhendu glanced at Ameeta. "Stay still! Just don't move!" he commanded.

Ameeta did not dare to move. The other woman, almost drained of half her blood, lay writhing on the floor.

Dr. Schmidt moved in leaping at Ardhendu. Ardhendu caught him mid-air by his throat. The other vampire, still down, was just beginning to get up. Seeing this, he froze.

Dr. Schmidt stared, the shock numbing his responses. Slowly, Ardhendu's nails began to cut into the vampire's throat.

The vampire screamed. This time, in terror.

The nails cut through the vampire's jugular vein. The other one jumped to his feet. His jaw was broken. He lurched at Ardhendu. Without looking at him, Ardhendu reached out and grabbed him by the throat too, his nails digging into his neck. Blood, rich and red, began to spurt from their throats. He lowered the other, forcing both to the ground. He knelt on the floor holding down the two struggling vampires who were now scratching at his hands, trying to break free. His nails dug deeper. Slowly there was recognition in Dr. Schmidt's terrified eyes.

Ardhendu's dark, expressionless visage was what the two carried out with them from this world.

When they stopped struggling, he drew out his switchblades, plunging them into their chests, one by one. The vampires were now truly dead. The silver infected their hearts swiftly, reducing them to lifeless lumps.

He walked over to Ameeta, who was trembling with fear and shock. "Go." He said simply.

"Y…you…" Recognition flickered in her eyes.

"Leave at once."

The girl fled instantly.

Ardhendu inspected the other girl who lay on the ground. Bloodless, almost lifeless. She looked at Ardhendu with pleading eyes. Ardhendu knelt down. He brought his hand down to her eyes and shut them. Then, with a swift, sweeping motion, he brought his switchblade down, beheading her.

He made it painless.

13

"Are you saying they were killed?"

Michelle nodded. Ramesh Tyagi stood by her side.

"Who gave them permission to hunt?" White roared.

"No one! They got carried away, I guess."

"I had made it clear. No hunting, not here in India. For Chrissake, with our R&D lab going, we needn't hunt at all. This company was formed so that humans could be served to us on a platter..."

"Yes, I know, but we're predators after all, the thrill of the hunt is difficult to control." Michelle's tone was bland.

"Then they deserve what happened to them..."

"Except, the way they were killed..."

"What way?"

"Whoever killed them, knew three things: they were vampires; what kills vampires and, more importantly...that he was more powerful and stronger than them."

Colton White turned around at the last sentence.

"Have the police been managed?" He addressed this query to Ramesh.

He nodded.

"Send out a press release immediately about how we poor foreigners are being targeted by criminals, etc. You said the guy took their watches and money?"

Ramesh nodded again.

"Press murder-with-an-intention-to-steal charges."

Ramesh was taking notes now.

"And find out who this fella is. When you do, I will go after him."

✧

"So. Colton White, the India head will meet you tomorrow."

The unsuspecting young management graduate thanked Ramesh Tyagi profusely.

"See you at 8 pm!"

They shook hands.

Ramesh Tyagi got up from his chair and headed towards the restroom. He relieved himself for a full five minutes. "This bloody diabetes!" He swore to himself. Washing his hands, he stared at his thirty-four-year-old visage in the mirror. "Man, I look forty-eight." He muttered to himself.

"You will look ninety-eight when I am done with you." Ardhendu's visage appeared beside his in the mirror.

Tyagi stared unbelievingly.

"Still serving humans on a platter to RED?"

Ramesh opened his mouth to say something but no words came out.

Ardhendu's gloved hand appeared on his shoulder in the mirror. It pulled him back, throwing him hard against the wall behind him. His senses shaken by the pain, Tyagi sat on the floor, his back to the wall, shock draining him of any response. He found his voice again when Ardhendu kneeled in front of him.

"Please, I'm sorry...please don't kill me!"

Ardhendu caught him by the throat, lifting him with one hand until Tyagi's feet dangled in the air.

"You're a diabetic, right?"

He made a choking noise with a horrified look in his eyes.

"All I need to do is make a little incision on your thigh. It will never heal. Soon you'll need an amputation."

"No, please!" Tyagi pleaded.

"I need a lowdown on all of RED's employees in India, now."

Tyagi was singing now, like a parrot.

Ardhendu listened attentively. He spoke only when Tyagi was completely done.

"OK, I won't kill you, at least not now. But I do need a favour."

"Yes, yes anything." Relief was palpable in Tyagi's voice.

"Tell Colton White that I killed his bloodsuckers. Tell him to begin counting."

Ardhendu walked towards the window of the restroom.

"You may call in the cops now!"

Tyagi's scream for help could be heard from a mile.

The cops burst in. Seeing Ardhendu, they began to draw their pistols. Ardhendu ran towards them. Seeing that, the cops were thrown out of gear. He stopped short, turning around and began to run towards the window. Without losing momentum, he dived. His body sliced through the glass cleanly like a blade cutting through grass, shooting out like an arrow before dropping sixteen stories down. On the first floor, he grabbed a light post by the road, and broke his fall. Then he swung his body right around it, landing with a somersault on the roof of the building next to it.

The cops opened fire.

Ardhendu began to run.

He jumped on reaching the end of the terrace.

A volley of gunfire greeted him at that end. Five police gypsies stood on the road. The constables were positioned well behind them. They fired leisurely at the fleeing figure.

A hot flash of fire shot through his left shoulder. A second one seared his left thigh. He ignored them, concentrating on the run. His legs twinkled as they took him at great speed into a culvert. Then he jumped, catapulting himself into the air. Turning mid-air, he landed on the top of the wall with his hands. Then he used his arms to propel himself once again; he landed neatly on his feet, rolling himself immediately to avoid the total impact on his now bleeding shoulder. He picked himself up, pulling out a piece of cloth from within his jacket and tied it around his thigh as he ran.

The sirens of the police vans were all around him. He jumped straight into the traffic on the Moolchand flyover. A DTC bus approached on the other side of the flyover. Ardhendu ran through the traffic as cars screeched around him, jumping neatly off a speeding Skoda, using his foot to nimbly land on a Maruti 800, denting its roof. Without waiting, he leapt right on to the railings of the flyover and then landed neatly on the roof of the DTC bus. The cops had reached the flyover by now. They took aim.

Sub-inspector Anuj Kumar barked. "Hold your fire!"

The constables stopped. "There are civilians here for God's sake. The press will screw us!"

He whipped out the walkie-talkie. "DTC bus number DL 1C 2016. He's on the roof. It's headed towards Maharani Bagh. Get him. Over!"

Ardhendu observed the scenario around him. The barricade was around half a kilometre away. The traffic was heavy at this time. However, as he looked behind, he could see two gypsies hot in pursuit. He didn't waste any time. So he jumped from the rooftop of the DTC bus onto the top of a Scorpio, and slipped.

He landed hard on the ground. The pavement was a yard away. Ignoring the pain, he got up and ran towards it. The passers-by screamed. It felt as if two hot knives were working their way through his shoulder and thigh. His top half was now quite bloody. But he ran. He turned left on a lane, ducking into a cluster of trees, then allowed himself a minute, to catch his breath.

"Udhar gaya!"

He heard the cops, and ran again.

A Mitsubishi Pajero drove up stealthily to him. Ardhendu panted now as he ran. As he passed the SUV, the driver's window rolled down.

"Mr. Bose. Get in here."

Ardhendu stopped suddenly. He turned around.

A black man sat at the wheel. He spoke in an African-American accent. "Mr. Bose, quick, get in here. I only wish to help you."

The earnestness in the man's voice made Ardhendu approach the SUV.

"Please get in. We'll talk inside. Please do it fast, before the cops get here."

It was one of those instantaneous decisions which we humans take in our lives. Ardhendu got in. The man keyed the ignition and the SUV sprang to life. He began to head towards Maharani Bagh.

"They have a police barricade there."

"You didn't see the number plate; it's a diplomatic one. They ain't gonna stop us."

They didn't.

"There is a first-aid box in the glove compartment. It has a disinfectant. Your shoulder and thigh need it."

Ardhendu helped himself.

"OK, where to?"

A switchblade flashed out in an instant, resting itself at the black man's throat.

"Who are you?"

The black man replied calmly, "Damon Broadus. CIA. The ID's on the dashboard. Take a look."

Ardhendu used his other hand to check it. "Why are you helping me?"

"Mr. Bose, the CIA has had its sights on RED for almost ten years now. Periodically, every year, some of their employees disappear without a trace. Investigations reveal nothing. This began to occur when they diversified into Europe and Canada too. Unfortunately, we haven't been able to prove anything about them.

"When they announced their India plans, I volunteered to come here, solely to keep an eye on their activities. You were their first reported disappearance. Ever since, I have been keeping tabs. I chose not to believe the charges levelled against you about those dancers. Why? Maybe, because I have tracked their activities long enough to know that they are definitely up to something very suspicious. What? I don't know. When two of their personnel got killed, I began my surveillance on them again. You appeared today and the police gave you chase. So I am here to understand from you what this is all about."

Pain had dulled Ardhendu's senses by now. "You've heard about vampires?"

"Er, yeah."

"That's them."

Broadus did not hide his smile. "Mr. Bose, this is not the time for jokes, you will need to be open with me..."

"I know. You have a dossier of all the people who have disappeared while on the rolls of RED in the past twenty odd years?"

"Yes, I do."

"Remember an Indian called Dr. Amitava Bose?"

"Yes, I do, University of Kansas, 1988."

"Wanna meet him?"

The smile on Broadus's face disappeared.

☙

Amitava ran towards his son as he appeared at the door. He nodded at Broadus, deciding that pleasantries could be exchanged later. His trained doctor's eyes took in the details as he laid his son down on the bed. He quickly examined his wounds. "You've lost a lot of blood." He observed. "Your bone marrow production has slowed down; the injection would not work under these circumstances. You'll have to do something else."

"What?" Ardhendu asked, his senses reeling.

"You'll have to ingest some blood."

Damon stiffened.

Ardhendu looked up at his father. "I... I will not do that," he said firmly.

"I'm afraid you have to, son. You don't have a choice."

"We all have a choice. My choice is that I will die but not ingest human blood; it doesn't matter whether or not I am a vampire."

Damon stood still watching the exchange. He decided not to interrupt.

Amitava ignored the comment. He took out a tube attached to a pin and pricked himself in the arm. His blood flowed out into the tube into a pouch. He waited ten minutes in silence as the pouch became half full. He poured the blood into a glass with one hand as he took the pin out of his arm with the other. He held the area of insertion expertly with his thumb and forefinger to stem the flow. Then he approached his son. "Your mother has sustained your life from a baby to an infant by making you consume her milk. That milk was created from her own blood. Therefore, I, as a father can very willingly offer you some of mine to sustain yours." He held out the glass.

Anjali and Damon watched, horrified.

Ardhendu stared at his dad; he felt an animalistic love for the man. He could blindly die for the man, blindly kill for the man. If anyone ever tried to hurt his father, he would tear him to shreds.

Amitava understood his son's feelings instinctively. He understood Ardhendu was not human anymore. Amitava approached him. He put his palm gently behind his son's ears, scratching his head. Like any other predator, this action began to ease Ardhendu's stress. He began to relax. Amitava held the glass under his nose. The scent of blood began to fill Ardhendu's nostrils. It was heady, intoxicating…it seemed almost lusty for him…he smelled deeply. Then it hit him…

"No!" He hissed, "I can't do this. Not your blood. I cannot." He pulled himself up from his bed.

Amitava continued to scratch the back of his ears. In a soothing voice he murmured, "It's OK son, it's ok...just do it." He continued to hold the glass under his son's nose. Ardhendu was torn between the desire to grab the glass, sink his molars in it and ingest the blood deep into his jugular vein, and the crippling feeling of intense disgust at the very same action! He shook, he burned and then in one definitive moment, he grabbed the glass and sunk his mouth into it. All sorts of hitherto unfelt sensations filled him as the blood ran into his jugular veins, staining his mouth, tongue, teeth and his nose. He did not stop until the glass was drained. It was as if a delicious insanity had taken hold of him. Finally, he put the glass down, staring at the people in the room...his eyes were wide open, glassy and bloodshot.

"Son, calm down," his father said softly, his fingers still scratching the back of his ears. Ardhendu turned around and looked deeply into his father's eyes. Slowly the impact of what he had done sank in. The grin disappeared and in its place a look of extreme sorrow and disgust filled his visage. He stared at the glass in his hand. Then he raised it and smashed it hard on the floor along with the last vestiges of humanity that had ever existed in him.

⟡

Broadus waved off the coffee and opted for whisky instead. He looked like he needed it.

Amitava had finished bandaging Ardhendu's shoulder by now. "I will give you the injection in an hour so that your bone marrow begins to produce itself again. The blood ingestion would have stimulated it by then. So, what's the plan?" he asked cheerfully.

Broadus took a deep breath.

"Mr. Bose, technically, in India, I am powerless. I report to the American Ambassador, who has agreed for my presence here, solely on the understanding that I restrict my role here to that of an observer. I am strictly forbidden to take any action. The geo-political situation being what it is, the US government is very keen on the nuclear deal becoming a success. Any CIA activity on this soil, if known, will screw things up. My posting here, on paper is more for security intelligence purposes in case someone poses a physical threat to the Ambassador."

"So, what you're saying is that you can't do a thing?"

"On paper, I can't."

"Then have we wasted your time?"

"Not at all. I need evidence to expose them. If I can work with your son, I can gather enough evidence to prove that they are…"

"Not some weird cult as you believed, but vampires." Amitava Bose finished his sentence.

"Ur, um yes…"

"So be it. But we'll do that, in exchange for your help."

"What's that?"

"Guns. RED has got their elite bodyguards from Europe in here. We have reason to believe that these are the legendary vampire fighting forces…"

"Er, can we call them something else…?"

Amitava Bose grinned. "Still having difficulty believing that they are vampires, eh? Don't worry, you'll soon be convinced. Anyway, to battle them we need semi-automatic weapons. I can have the silver bullets made. Also, we need some Kevlar."

"Kevlar?"

"So that my son does not get shot up anymore."

The two sat silently staring at each other.

"Well?"

"Yeah, I could have some delivered to you through the mercenaries we employ here. Only don't ask me what they do."

"I don't really care, anyway."

"OK. You'll have the Kevlar and a couple of semi-automatics by this weekend. In return, I go along with your son to gather evidence about their..."

"...bloodsucking!" Amitava finished his sentence.

Broadus kept quiet.

"It's a deal." Amitava offered his hand. Broadus accepted it gingerly. Amitava burst into laughter while Broadus stared at him curiously.

"Are you aware of your antecedents?"

Broadus was a little taken aback at this personal question, more so, as it was a non-American who had asked it. But he thought it fit to answer. "Well, I am told that my great grandfather was a slave who escaped from a tobacco plantation in Maryland in 1850 and settled somewhere in Arizona in a mining town called Tombstone..."

"Where the gunfight at the OK Corral happened..." Amitava interjected.

"Yes, my father was a rancher and I chose to go to college at New York State University..."

Amitava burst into laughter.

Broadus stared at him curiously.

Ardhendu looked up too.

Amitava turned to his wife, who sat motionless by her son.

"It's funny, now if you look at it..."

"Er, what?"

"A brown and a black man join hands to fight a team of white people who are hell bent on taking over this world. Sounds like one of those cheap race reruns on HBO, doesn't it?"

Broadus looked on as the reality of that statement sunk in. Visions of what he had read in books on slavery in America raced through his mind. The analogy was not lost on him. He grinned, albeit for the first time during this conversation, and indeed at perhaps the oddest and most remarkable day in his life so far.

Ardhendu remained impassive through this exchange.

Anjali Bose, on the other hand, sat there, her eyes glazed over with horror.

14

"So it was him, you're sure. And you're saying that he seems to be stronger, more agile and even highly aggressive?"

"Actually, he was really scary like…like…"

"…us?" Colton White concluded Tyagi's utterance.

"You told him about all our people?"

"Er, yes, otherwise he would have killed me."

"I understand. You've done well Tyagi, you need your rewards. Michelle!" He called out.

Michelle entered his room.

"Give him his reward!" White walked out.

Tyagi's eyes grew wide as Michelle approached him seductively. She flicked her finger over his face. "Hey there, baby! Want some American pie?"

Tyagi salivated.

Michelle pulled him to her.

Tyagi stared at Michelle expectantly, his eyes shining like two bright moons.

She took his head in her hands, bringing his face up to hers. He went like an infant to its mother.

She smiled at him sweetly. Then she opened her mouth wide, displaying her canines. In a sweeping motion, she grabbed his hair, pulling his head back. He looked at her all fired up by now. Then he saw her molars. "No, please!" He begged.

She tore his Adam's apple out with her teeth. He struggled as he choked upon himself in her arms. She sank her teeth in his neck as he thrashed about pitifully. When she was satiated, she dropped him unevenly.

Choking on himself, Tyagi watched the last dance of his own body's horrific death.

✧

Jude Young, the fifty-four-year-old proprietor of Young Brothers did not bat an eyelid when Ardhendu walked in. He continued to serve the existing customers in his small little shoe shop. Rows of footwear lined the walls. Some fine ornately carved riding boots shone in the dull light of the tube. The inside of the store had the untidy look which this made-to-order Chinese shoe man was proud of. His was a studio where he himself would get his hands dirty making the shoes and boots for customers who had patronised this store since the fifties.

Ardhendu stood in a corner, unmoving, almost blending into the surroundings of the store.

At exactly 1 pm, Jude Young turned the American Express sign on his door around. It said 'Closed for Lunch'. He bolted it and pulled a curtain across the display window. Then he acknowledged Ardhendu with a faint nod.

Going back to his counter, he took out a box. Placing it on the table, he removed its lid. He pulled out some of the paper on it and brought out two pieces of clothing.

Ardhendu stood still.

"The leather is sewn over the Kevlar. It will stop bullets, but I would not take chances with a .45 magnum," said Jude, matter-of-factly.

The black leather jacket was a good fit. Ardhendu pulled the leather wrap around his jeans. It was styled in the fashion of old-time ranch hands, fitting snugly over his legs.

Jude pulled out two belts of cartridges from the box. "You put this through the loops of the inners, and it goes around your waist." Expertly, he passed the belt through the loops. "And this one is on your back."

Ardhendu allowed the man to fix his suit.

Now Jude pulled out another box, smaller in size. "Managed to forge around three hundred with the silver your father gave me. This should last you for a while?"

Ardhendu nodded, opening the box. The silver in the cartridges made them shine in the dull light. He placed them in his jacket.

Without a word, he turned away.

"Your father and I went to school together. You tell him to watch his behind."

Ardhendu said in his low growling voice, "I shall," and walked out into the sunlight, his glares shielding his deep blue eyes from incredulous looks of the passers-by. He strode across the promenade and into the parking lot. The December sun cast a comforting glow on the passers-by who walked hand-in-hand, into the restaurants and the various stores in the inner circle of Connaught Place.

Ardhendu took large strides down the road along the inner circle. Traffic was still manageable today; he began to walk on the sides.

Two Kawasaki Ninjas sped past him. The riders were clad from head to toe in leather. They wore dark helmets. They turned to look at him, and let out loud whoops! As they faded in the distance, another motorcycle, with a pillion rider slowed down next to him. The pillion rider held a box neatly gift wrapped, in his hands. Both riders were clad from head to toe in leather; they wore gloves and dark helmets.

The pillion rider called out to Ardhendu in a low American accent. "Hey, vampire killer!"

Ardhendu stopped. He was not carrying any of his weapons as it was daytime.

"With compliments from RED." He shoved the box in Ardhendu's hands, and the riders began to speed away.

Ardhendu deftly unwrapped the covers. It was a wooden box which said 'Bunnahabhain 18 years'. The wood was fine mahogany. He opened the lid. Fine cloth lined the box in which stood the gift. Crystal's head lay neatly severed on the expensive cloth. The blood on the remnants of her neck had begun to congeal. Her face was serene, her tongue hanging out a bit as she slept a deep sleep.

In the distance, the riders let out loud whoops.

Ardhendu looked up. They had now begun to go around the inner circle heading for the exit near Regal Cinema.

Ardhendu dropped the box and began to run.

In a few bounds he cleared the breadth of the road sprinting over the small fence of the park over Palika Bazaar. He dashed across the park, leaping over the benches lined across it. Young couples basking in the afternoon sunlight, gazed at him curiously. He reached the other side and leapt over the fence. He almost flew through the air, bringing his right foot forward while cocking his left. His right foot hit the pillion rider squarely on the head, knocking him instantly off the motorcycle. Unable to keep his balance, the rider skidded and fell. In complete shock, he tried to pick himself up. Ardhendu had landed neatly on his feet by this time. He fell on the pillion rider, holding him by the neck, and pulled off the helmet with the other. There was fear in the deep blue eyes of the rider as the helmet came off. The sun was now at its peak. Ardhendu caught him by the hair, exposing his face to it. The man screamed. Smoke formed in his eyes first, and then his hair caught fire. Ardhendu dropped him, sprinting towards the rider who was trying to get his bike up. Ardhendu caught him by the collar, jerking him back. The smell told him that it was a human. Ardhendu mounted the bike; he turned it around in the traffic, dragging the man by his collar with his left hand. A Blue Line bus appeared behind him. Ardhendu let go.

The bus's wheels did the rest.

The two bikers ahead had seen what had happened. They opened throttle, riding out full force to towards Regal Cinema. Ardhendu followed on the bike. People began to flock to the footpaths to watch the spectacle.

Riding out from Regal Cinema, they turned right on the outer circle, merging with the traffic; they took a left from Barakhamba to Ashoka Road. They looked back; the vampire slayer was nowhere to be seen. They got on to the Purana Quila Road, towards the Ring Road, crossed Maharani Bagh and headed to the Delhi-Noida flyway. They were riding at around 100 kmph on the Greater Noida expressway. The road cut right across verdant fields. It was only then that they noticed another Kawasaki Ninja, bounding at them through the fields.

Ardhendu nudged the bike on to the side road, allowing its front wheel to graze lightly on the surface as he maneuvered it up the slope. He changed gears to the third, giving it an additional burst of power. The bike shot across the side, froze briefly in mid-air and landed on its rear, a few metres behind the other two riders.

The two riders pulled out their guns.

The Kevlar did the job. The bullets bounced off. Ardhendu did not bother to duck. Within minutes he rode his bike between the two; he took his hands off the handle and grabbed both off them by the collars, yanking them neatly off their bikes. The bikes skidded and fell ahead. Ardhendu stopped his. He walked back to the two who were trying to get up. He kicked one in the chest, crunching his ribs, then picked the other's foot up, and twisting it quickly. The bone snapped into two. The vampires screamed in agony.

The crops swayed gently in the breeze. The afternoon sun shone brilliantly on the three figures in the middle of a vast field. The vampires lay still, not daring to move. Ardhendu observed them from head to toe. They wore dark leather, with thick dark helmets. Not even the smallest rays of the sun would penetrate their attire. He pulled out his switchblades.

Then grabbing one of the riders, he ripped through the leather pants at the thighs. With a flourish, he pulled them off.

The vampire screamed as his legs began to burn.

Ardhendu did the same with the other rider. He then ripped off the sleeves of their jackets.

The vampires screamed in agony as the sun began its merciless onslaught on their arms and legs.

Ardhendu stood there as the sun reduced their arms and legs to ashes.

They lay there with their helmets on, wasting away.

Ardhendu turned and walked away. By the time he had reached his bike, they were begging him to kill them off.

15

Manoj had just finished his shift. He walked down to his Santro, and began to drive away. Ardhendu followed in his car, keeping good distance. Manoj swerved right on the Sector 55 crossing at Noida, then drove on to Sector 40, where he turned right to take the shortcut to the Greater Noida expressway.

In about 20 minutes, he had reached Eldeco Residency Greens. The watchmen waved him in. Ardhendu drove back, and parked his car near the Golf Course. He moved silently on foot and scaled the back wall of Eldeco Residency Greens; he now followed Manoj's scent.

Right near the back gate, he saw Manoj get off and walk into one of the four-storied buildings in the compound. Manoj took the stairs to the 2nd floor and rang the bell.

Ardhendu climbed the pipe silently to the second floor. His dark clothes aided by the inky darkness of the night, shielded him from prying eyes. He peered through the window.

A woman's voice wafted through.

"Any news of Crystal?"

"No, none, I have lodged a complaint with the cops today."

"Where could she have gone?"

"I really have no idea."

A woman in a night suit came out of a room inside. She had her back to the window. She knelt down and hugged Manoj, who turned his face up and kissed her cheek.

"How's the baby doing?"

"Slept soundly today. So, I could catch up on sleep too."

"Good for you, sweetheart!" Manoj said.

Ardhendu felt something stir within him. He looked carefully through the window. He did not expect this unwanted interruption. He had wished to contact Manoj one on one, so he could appraise him of the fact that Crystal was kidnapped and killed by the vampires and he could be next. But he did not want to do so in front of this woman, whoever she was. He would end up scaring her. Contacting Manoj during the day or in public view would put his life in danger. Then the woman turned in the direction of Ardhendu, her face now visible. He stared at her, his blue eyes unblinking. The gait, the skin and the voice flung him back into his past. He clenched his teeth as something inside him began to boil.

The baby was awake now. Veena walked back into the bedroom and lifted him, cooing gently into his ears, "Daddy's back."

Ardhendu had had enough. He let go of the pipe and dropped gently to the ground.

〰️

"Did you meet him?" Amitava Bose asked without looking up.

"No."

"He is going to be in danger. You need to protect him."

"No."

Amitava Bose looked at his son. "I thought he is your best friend."

Ardhendu did not answer.

Amitava looked at him quizzically.

"He married her."

Anjali Bose, who was sitting quietly, as usual, went up to her son. "Oh, Ardhendu, I am so sorry." She put her arms around him.

Ardhendu pulled away, standing motionless in a corner. She was not supposed to touch him, but would a mother ever remember that.

"Son, whatever be the case, you can't let them be in danger like this."

Ardhendu turned around. His cold blue eyes piercing his mother's in a predatory gaze. His voice was low and guttural.

"I don't care."

"My God, how can you say that? What have you become?" Anjali Bose moaned.

Ardhendu waited for his mother to recover. When she did, he spoke softly, "I was never aggressive enough for you, was I? Now see what I have become!" Then he sneered, his canines glowing in the faint light of the warehouse.

Anjali Bose stared in shock at this ghastly sight. Tears streamed from her eyes.

The elder Bose sat still in his chair; his cigar had just gone off. He reached out for the matchbox to light it again.

"Leave him alone, Anjali," he said quietly. Anjali turned and looked at him. A slow realisation dawned on her. Her son was no longer hers. She sighed. And then, stooped. In the dark of the room it looked as though she had suddenly aged. She stood like that, unmoving, resting a hand on the wall for support. Neither her son, nor her husband came up to offer any help. Then she walked out of the room, haltingly and with a stoop that she would now carry for the rest of her life.

The two watched her leave, allowing her to reflect on her emotions and insights in her own private world.

"Aren't you going to sleep?"

Amitava Bose ignored the question. He was working hard on the laptop. "Here, look at this."

Ardhendu walked up to him. The screen showed 'Banque Nationale de Paris'. Beneath it was a small table. Inside that was an account. It read, 'Transfer of 4,000,000 Euros from RED, France to RED, India'.

Amitava typed furiously on the keyboard. The screen went blank. Then it lit up again: 'Transfer rerouted', then 'New transfer initiated'. Then the screen said, 'Transferring'.

Amitava turned around to Ardhendu, a faint smile on his lips. "I have just rerouted 4 million Euros to an undisclosed account in Switzerland."

"Whose?"

"Mine."

"How?"

"I hacked into RED's accounts. It took me three months. Now those suckers will have no money for their operations in India." He ejected the CD from his laptop and handed it to Ardhendu. "Keep this. It has details of all my different accounts in India and abroad. There must be around 10 million dollars stashed away in them. All money stolen from RED. I have given you exclusive access to these accounts. It's all yours.

Use it wisely in our war against these bloodsuckers." There was no trace of guilt in his voice. Then he broke into laughter.

"It's funny. These two-legged parasites have funded the very war that we have launched against them!"

16

Manoj shifted uncomfortably in his seat. The movie was another mindless romance. The baby broke into a wail. Veena looked at him beseechingly. Almost thankfully, Manoj scooped up the little infant in his arms and walked out to the lobby of the multiplex. A couple nodded at him sympathetically. He shrugged his shoulders and smiled at them. Holding the baby close to his chest, he hummed gently into its ears. The baby fell silent in minutes. Manoj decided that it was better to order a soft drink in the lobby than to face the brutality of the song and dance extravaganza inside the hall. He sat on the steps of the lobby, cradling the baby, staring at his beautiful features. The infant looked back at him, his face bathed in a smile, holding up his little fingers. Manoj let him feel his face. The baby did so in innocent wonder.

"You're a good father!" He looked up. It was an American woman. She was accompanied by an American man. Dressed in mall clothes (jeans and T-shirts), they stood smiling at him.

"Why, thanks!" Manoj smiled back.

"Can we look at him?" The woman asked.

"Sure."

The two stared at the little baby, marvelling at his innocent beauty. "You're such a lucky man! He's beautiful!"

"Thanks."

"Where's his mom?" She asked.

"Oh, she's inside watching the horror flick."

The man burst out laughing. "I know what you're talking about. I couldn't take that torture anymore!"

"So, have you guys been here long?"

"Oh, we got to India about a month ago. Thought we'll take in the local culture, so we came to see this movie. They say it's a big hit."

"Well, they say that people will pay to be scared." Manoj stabbed the movie's poster with his thumb: two newcomers in outrageous costumes stood in a dancing pose. The heroine had assumed a coquettish pose, while the hero, smiled a movie-star smile, displaying his dentist's expertise.

The man laughed easily as the woman joined him.

"Daniel, and this one here answers to the name of Joanna." The man stuck his palm out.

Manoj grabbed it warmly, "Manoj."

"Say, any place here where we can grab a beer?"

"Oh there's a pub on this floor. You could get some lager on tap there."

"Oh good! We'll head that way. Say, would you like to join us?"

Manoj smiled. "Why, sure. But my wife's inside…"

"Well, why don't you tell her to join us there once the movie is done?"

"Good idea! Would you give me a minute?" Manoj sprinted in and out in less than a minute. "Let's get the heck out of here!"

"Sure," said Daniel.

They were on their third pitcher when Veena walked in.

"Hey there, gorgeous!" Manoj reached out to kiss his wife on the cheek.

"I'd like to avoid the beer breath today honey, if that's OK."

Daniel and Joanna laughed.

"What would you like?"

"Oh, a Margarita would be fine."

Veena took the baby on her lap. "Do you need a nappy change, pumpkin? Yes, you do. Trust Daddy to forget..."

"Oh, I am sorry, I was..."

"...drinking your beer, yes I know." Veena sighed. "Guys, I'll be right back."

The merry-making continued until closing time.

The Americans insisted on paying.

"Say, how would you guys be going home? Do you have any transport?"

"No, but we'll hail a cab."

"Well, where are you guys staying?"

"Oh, at The Park, near Connaught Place."

"Can I drop you there?"

"Oh, no," Joanna said, "that would be out of your way, right? You said you live in Greater Noida?"

"Oh, no that's fine. It's not safe for the two of you to be taking a cab at this hour. We'll drop you to Connaught Place."

"Are you sure?"

"Yes, of course!" Veena said.

They got into the elevator and rode down to the dimly lit basement parking.

They were on Man Singh Road when it happened.

A Scorpio with its headlights off passed them by and then swerved on the road, blocking their path. Manoj braked hard. Joanna had the baby in her arms. She jerked forward, shielding the baby instinctively.

"What the…?" Daniel started.

The seat belts held back Manoj and Veena tightly.

A man got off from the Scorpio. He had a handkerchief tied across his face. It was not the kerchief that worried Manoj as much as the Winchester .22 bore rifle the man carried in his hand. He had it aimed at the car and began to advance. Manoj could barely make out the other man sitting inside.

"Alright, the two of you, get out of that friggin' car." The man barked.

Manoj, beckoned to Veena, "Let's just do what he says…"

"Not you, I am talking to those trailer trashes sitting behind, out there."

Daniel and Joanna stared in shock.

The man advanced holding his rifle steady. "Now hand over that baby, nice and easy to the woman in front. Do it, now!"

Joanna stared without moving.

"Listen Sir, we don't mean any harm, please…" Manoj said.

"Quiet, son! I ain't talking to you."

The man advanced towards the car, his rifle aimed at Joanna. "Listen, sweetheart! This Winchester has been loaded with special bullets: Grade A silver. You know what's going to happen when I plug one right in? Now the baby…"

"Yeah? What cha gonna do, cowboy?" Joanna's mouth opened. Her fangs glowed in the streetlight. She brought them close to the baby's head. "Take a step closer and I turn this pathetic piece of flesh into a geyser."

Daniel smiled too. His fangs glinted in the light. Manoj and Veena turned around. Their eyes grew wide seeing the transformation.

The baby began to wail...

"Ah, you suckers are always so predictable." Amitava Bose said sarcastically.

Damon had got off the SUV by now. He began to advance with his pistol drawn. He stared in shock at the woman's teeth.

"What are you doing? Give me back my baby..." Veena was hysterical by now.

Joanna struck her across the face.

Veena's head hit the window of her door. Blood oozed from her mouth.

Manoj turned around. "Hey..."

Daniel struck Manoj on his face, sending him flying back towards the dashboard.

"Friggin' humans! You dare mess with us?" he roared.

"Yes," said Amitava, simply Then, he squeezed the trigger. The bullet sailed neatly into Joanna's open mouth. It tore open her tonsils and exited through the back of her neck. The silver acted quickly.

"The baby, quick!" Amitava motioned to Veena. Instinctively, Veena grabbed her infant, opened the door, stumbled out and ran towards Amitava.

Manoj sat in shock as Daniel grabbed him from behind to shield himself.

Joanna screamed, her face turning blue. A severe allergic reaction set in. Her face swelled several times and she was unable to breathe. Then her skull burst open, sending pieces of her flying around inside the car.

That's when the rest of them arrived. Fifteen of them, dropping from trees, buildings and alleys. Dressed in black, with their weapons.

"Oh, crap! It's the back-up," he told Damon. "Get the girl and the baby in the car, we gotta move."

"But the guy, he's still there."

"I know, but we don't stand a chance."

"But…"

"Believe me. We gotta go." Amitava backed off into the SUV, not letting his rifle down. The vampires advanced gingerly, not wanting to take the silver bullets. Manoj looked up beseechingly from the windshield of his car. Damon bundled Veena and the baby in. She was sobbing uncontrollably.

෴

Ardhendu watched silently.

"You have to save him."

"No." He replied.

"Ardhendu, he is your best friend."

"That's why he married her?" Ardhendu pointed his finger at Veena.

Veena glared at him. "Yes he did, knowing full well that I was pregnant."

Ardhendu stopped in his tracks.

"That the child was not his; it is yours." Veena completed her sentence quietly.

Ardhendu went blank for a moment. There was a perceptible quiet in the air. Amitava sat silently. Anjali Bose had her hand on Veena's shoulder. Damon wished he was someplace else.

Anjali Bose picked up the infant. She carried it and offered it to Ardhendu. Ardhendu shrank back.

"This is your child for heaven's sake. You should hold him once."

Ardhendu's fangs glinted in the soft light of the warehouse. "Keep him away from me!" He snarled.

"What's the matter with you? He's your son…"

"Don't you understand? He could get infected if I touch him!" Ardhendu reached for the staircase, trying hard to keep his emotions in check. Minutes later, in the small room upstairs, staring at the dusty mirror, he smote it with his bare fist, smashing it to pieces. He picked up a piece of glass and held it over his palm. He drove the piece slowly into it. He stood there unmoving, watching the blood flow from the wound as the glass lay embedded, its bloody end protruding from the bottom of his palm. He stood there for a long time and then pulled it out. Pain was good, it helped take his mind away from the bottomless pit of self-loathing.

It was early morning. The wound was healing; his cells would always multiply faster. He heard the drums in the distance…the old familiar beat of the *dhak*. He went outside.

His mother stood there. "You heard it too?"

He stared at her blankly.

"Today is Shashti. The first day of Durga Pooja. Remember how you used to love the Poojas? I would take you to Matri Mandir, Acharya Mukul would give us the first prasad…"

Ardhendu remembered. It seemed like another lifetime. The human in him went back to those days, the first onset of winter, the sun no longer a biting ball of fire…the sweet smell of *bhog*, the new clothes, the chatter of Bengali women, the pretty girls at the pandals, dressed in their finest, the succulent rolls… the musical performances…the…

Then the bitter truth stared him in the face…he would never see them again. Those days and that festival were for humans, not a predator…

⌒

"It's settled then. You will drive from here to Calcutta; leave your mother, Veena and the child in my ancestral home at Sreerampur. Once you are back, the three of us will take on RED."

Ardhendu nodded and got into the SUV with Veena, the baby and his mother. He turned to his father. "Be careful."

"Don't worry." Amitava Bose nodded. Damon nodded too.

Ardhendu waved at both, then drove off.

As the SUV sped into the distance, Damon turned to Amitava. "Aren't you worried?"

"About what?"

"That Ardhendu could attack you, sometime?"

"Does a Rottweiler ever attack its master?"

Damon nodded in understanding.

They reached Sreerampur three days later. Veena and Anjali observed that Ardhendu did not speak a word during the entire journey. He stole glances at his boy from time to time. Other than that, his face showed no emotion.

On reaching the farm, he spoke briefly to the caretaker. He looked once at his mother and Veena and then got back into the SUV.

"Ardhu, will I ever see you again, son?" Anjali asked him as he began to switch on the ignition. Ardhendu looked at her without answering. He wanted to head back to Delhi. He had a greater task to fulfil. So he drove off silently.

Anjali watched the dust the wheels of the SUV raised as it hurtled down the road. She knew in her heart that she would never see him again. With a sigh, she slumped down on that road, drained, weary of life. She sat like that for a long time until Veena came to her and put an arm around her. "You still have someone to live for," she said.

Anjali raised her head and saw the innocent toothless grin of her grandson. She picked up the baby and cradled it to her bosom. And then she wept like a bereaved mother and a grateful grandmother. She would no longer make anything significant.

17

Amitava Bose took another look at the monkey in the cage. It was dead now. He looked away, shaking his head. The medicine was just not effective beyond a day. He typed his notes into the laptop. He switched on the laptop's camera and spoke into the mike. "The fact is, the vampire state cannot be altered. The medicine can only do so much to stimulate bone marrow production, but beyond that, nothing. Perhaps through this research, I could come up with a cure for cancer. Bose, out."

Then the alert flashed in the warehouse. There were twenty of them on the computer that monitored the webcams. Bose could tell by the way they moved. He switched off his laptop quickly and shoved it into the secret vault beneath the table. Then he picked up the automatic and a spare cartridge belt.

Colton White motioned to the vampires. "Follow the bloody scent!"

"White! It's been a while. How the hell have you been?"

Amitava Bose now stood on the railing of the first floor.

"Good to see you, Bose. You've been bit of a pain, you know."

"Always! I aim to please!"

"You stole money from us, eh? Transferred funds from our French bank. We caught you. We traced you through our internet tracking mechanism as you accessed our accounts. You forget, we have sophisticated tracking tools!"

"Good for you, White. But you poor, friggin' fool! I have been stealing money from you for the past twenty years! You guys are certified idiots! I am a rich man and will leave enough for generations to come!"

"Yeah, but no more."

White signalled to the rest of the vampires. "Go after him! Get him! Alive!"

The vampires began to move ahead.

"It's dark in here, don't you think? I can't see your faces. Let there be some light." Bose pointed with his remote, then hit a button. The lights of the warehouse switched on. Hard, bright lights enveloped the vampires, their fluorescence shining on their faces. Many of them began to emit smoke.

"Ultra-violet rays!" White shouted. "Kill the lights!"

Ten of the vampires had already caught fire, their shrill screams of terror bouncing off the walls. Three of them aimed their carbines at the lights; it took a minute to get them all.

White looked up. Bose had disappeared.

✍

Bose opened the vault. He quickly pulled out a CD-ROM from his jacket and dropped it into a chute. Then he messaged Ardhendu the location. He began to run towards the trapdoor for the exit to the roof. Two vampires blocked his way; he fired at them. They fell to floor writhing as the silver began to eat up their insides.

He had barely reached the trapdoor when he noticed a vampire standing underneath it, waiting for him.

Bose turned back. The remaining vampires had lined up for him. He opened fire! And they returned it. One of them got his left shoulder. Bose fell to the ground. Then raising himself up again, he sat at the corner of the railing on the first floor. His shoulder bled profusely. Colton White stood in front of him, grinning. The endgame was near.

"You know what, Bose? We ain't gonna kill you. We are going to turn you into a vampire."

"You know what, White? You are not going to get that opportunity. Not, in this lifetime."

"Oh, hush! Let's cut the dialogue, right? You have just one bullet left, so what are you going to do, really?"

"Yeah. I have one bullet. But I'll put it to good use. Who wants to make the first move?" Bose was smiling now. "I have plenty of time."

The vampires waited. No one was willing to make the first move.

White shook his head. "Our differences were based on a moot point, Bose. We vampires too deserve our place in the world. Why should we live like fugitives, in hiding? Your race has never accepted us. You have hunted us down, and made us into these so-called monsters...you think that is fair? RED was formed so that our species would live. They would have clean blood to survive on...all I had asked you at that time, was to give us a hand. And you took it away..."

Bose did not allow him to finish. "Vampires are four times stronger, four times agile and perhaps even more intelligent than humans, right? So you guys create a company to purify blood… how come it never occurred to you to research on how to curb your blood thirst? Or are you too intelligent for that?" He laughed, although in pain. "The bane of this world has always been intelligence; it was a scientist, who created the nuclear bomb, you get it? Not an ordinary human being. Perhaps, White, you should have put your money into what would have allowed you to co-exist with humans, without the need to consume them. But no, that would never occur to you…you're too intelligent, sorry, an intellectual, right? Intellectualism is nothing but arrogance. You and your race have always been arrogant. If you had used your EQ instead of IQ, vampires and humans could always have co-existed. But no, you chose not to. You cannot live if your living is based on making someone else die."

White intervened, "Nature created us and simply made us superior!"

"Yes, but nature also made you guys inferior in many ways. Look at your allergies. Also, White, you think I do not know? Ninety per cent of vampires are sterile. You guys have trouble reproducing. That's why there are less than one hundred thousand vampires alive in this world! So you go about infecting people! Wow! That's intelligent, right? Ever occurred to you what would happen if you turned the entire human race into vampires? What would you eat then? Each other? Hah! You make me laugh!

"So humans have always occurred to you as poultry, right? Guess what? We're not. And this is not the place where you can pick and choose and create the slaves to serve your cause. No, we will fight back. You hear?"

Bose's words only made White angrier. "Bose, the odds are against you, you are going to miss…" he lunged towards Bose.

"No, I won't!" Bose said with a grin. He lifted his pistol with great difficulty, pulling the trigger only when the muzzle stood firmly at his own temple.

White roared with rage as he saw Bose collapse. He grabbed him by the collars and shook him, willing him to live, as it were. Bose's body began to shudder and in that final shuffle of his life, he winked at the vampire. Then his head fell to the side. He had exited honourably from this world.

White let him drop. He turned around and leaned against the wall. This was the second time in his life that he was defeated by this human and there was nothing he could have done about it. The taste of that defeat hung bitterly on his lips. So he spat, on the dead body. He fell upon it with a rage that was terrifyingly ferocious; kicking, pummelling, tearing away. He plunged his fingers into the stomach, reaching deep and yanking the intestines out. He broke an arm into two…by the time he was done, even he was horrified at the mutilation.

In the recesses of his mind, he began to feel a sense of shame at what he had done. After all, Bose had died an honourable death and he as a Prince had not respected that. So he covered the body with a sheet. He shook his head at the body, knowing full well that perhaps in another world and time, they could have been collaborators instead of adversaries.

⟡

The warehouse was completely destroyed. The test tubes lay smashed on the floor. The monkey lay impaled on a knife, hanging from the notice board. The lathe machines were overturned.

Ardhendu sifted through the mess, following the bloody trail. Then he sprinted up the ladder onto the railing of the first floor. A body lay there on the floor covered with a shroud. A pistol lay on the floor beside it. He peeled off the shroud… Amitava's open, unblinking eyes stared at nothingness. The congealed blood from the small hole in his temple drew a crooked rusty line down his face. Ardhendu looked silently at his father's battered body, the strewn intestines, the broken bones and the gouged flesh. Then he stood up. A fierce wind was whipping him with its icy lashes. His throat felt constricted; his head felt as though it would burst as grief ate away at him. The human in him sought release from pain, but that was not to be. There wasn't a single tear in his eyes. He held his father's lifeless body in his arms, staring up at the skies. The North Star had gone behind a cloud.

The moon rose slowly in the sky. Ardhendu knelt down, letting his father's body drop gently to the floor. He raised his head towards the moon, then opened his mouth with his fangs bared. With all his might, he willed his grief to find a voice. Deep from the recesses of his throat rose a growl. Then slowly it evolved into a long plaintive howl that pervaded the city. Pavement-dwellers shivered. A lone wolf stood in the ridge. It caught the howl and joined in. Street dogs caught the strains and joined in the chorus. They howled together, almost one with he who was no longer only human.

Residents of the buildings nearby began to draw the curtains, pull down blinds and shut their windows as the howls engulfed them like a thick fog.

The silver coin in the sky gazed down on them, receiving their ode silently.

Colton White's office was sound proof, but his keen ears heard the howls. He looked up, walked to his window, taking in the panoramic view of Connaught Place. In the distance, he saw the dogs howling in chorus.

A sudden chill went up his spine.

⤙

Ardhendu stood silently in front of the smashed mirror as he zipped up his jacket. He pulled on the covers of his jeans, zipping his boots soon after. He checked the foundry for the silver shells. He filled all of them in the belt loops. Then he cleaned his semi-automatic in silence. After that, he sharpened his switchblades. Placing them inside the jacket sheaths, he gathered the CD-ROM, tucking it carefully in one of jacket's inside pockets.

He looked around the warehouse one last time. Then he injected himself with the antivirus. He took the last test tubes and carefully tucked them into his pouch. Then he turned around and strode out. He took out a remote from his pocket and pressed a button on it. The roof caved in as he walked away, and the explosion erased everything his father had built over the years. Then he got into the SUV and drove off. He was in no hurry. He drove up to the cursed building in Connaught Place. Parking the SUV at a distance, he approached the building stealthily and started scaling it.

The climb was a long and arduous one. The wind whipped him mercilessly as he climbed the walls, grabbing small ledges and panes sometimes with his hands. Propelling himself with his feet, he reached the balcony of the thirtieth floor. Then he leaped. Grabbing the railing of the balcony, he catapulted himself into the balcony.

He used his switchblade to cut a small hole through the door, and put his hand through and opened the latch. The door opened noiselessly and Ardhendu stepped in.

The bedroom was dark and unoccupied. He moved out into the living room. There was no trace of the carnage that had occurred a year ago. He strode into the middle of the room. Nothing was out of place. Not a thing stirred.

It was then that the laser beam reflected in his eyes.

He stepped back. Colton White appeared in front of him instantly. He was relaxed, dressed in his finest Versace suit and his ornately designed boots. "Welcome Ardhendu. You have proved to be a worthy adversary. It's been decades since I have actually faced someone with even half your courage."

White paused for effect. "You've killed my men, and crippled my operations here. I, in turn, killed your dog, your father and now, I have your best friend with me. Not to mention, the country's police is after your blood. So, here's the deal: I have your best friend in the R&D lab at Uttaranchal. I plan to do interesting things with him. Very interesting things. If you want him free, come to the lab. Come alone and come unarmed. I plan to tie you up, tear you apart limb by limb as your friend watches. Finally, when you have just a little bit of life left, I will set him free. That I promise. But come, I will wait only for forty-eight hours. After that I plan to start working on your friend. Needless to say, I will work on him slowly and very painfully. Oh and..."

Ardhendu sprang at White and sailed through him, landing on the other side of the room.

"This is just a holographic image. If you want the real me, come to the lab. Use the underground escape tunnel. Don't keep me waiting now."

The image flickered and disappeared.

18

"Don't do it. It ain't worth it."

Ardhendu stood silently.

"I'm telling you man, it ain't worth it. He is going to kill Manoj anyway. He's just luring you there so that he can kill two birds with...you get the drift." Damon stood with the CD-ROM in his hand, observing the remnants of the warehouse.

"I know. But I'm going there."

"Listen, you've got your mother, Veena and the baby. I'd bail out with this. I can arrange it. I'll get you out of the country; bring your mother, Veena and the baby. I'll set you up with a new identity, somewhere in the Philippines. We'll regroup there with some of the CIA's mercenaries. It'll take some time, but we can do it. Once I convince my bosses in Washington, we'll develop a strategy to finish off these guys. In any case, I think we can start generating some heat for them through the media here.

"Through your father's research, I'm sure we can generate a dosage that lasts longer for your condition. We have the resources." Broadus waved the CD-ROM at Ardhendu. "The bottom line is that whatever we do, it will take some time, a few months. But once we do regroup, we can attack them in larger numbers, hitting them across the world. It'll be a war, but we can win it.

"Going there alone right now will be suicidal. It ain't worth risking your life for just one guy. We gotta look at the larger picture."

"I'm still going."

"Look man, the war with the vampires is not going to get over with just this one fight. This is an impossible fight; they can and will kill you. I cannot afford to lose you like this…"

"Why?"

"Because the CIA needs you. We need a mercenary to lead the war against the vampires. And it has to be you."

"Then get someone else. Because I am going there."

"But why?"

"My son needs a father."

Damon looked defeated. "So be it then, but you are going to your death."

Ardhendu turned around to face him. Then pointing to himself, he said, "You call this being alive?"

There was silence for a minute.

Damon broke it.

"In this day and age when courage, honour and valour seem to be words from the Jurassic, it is an honour to have known you." He stretched out his hand. Ardhendu gripped it firmly. Then he got into the SUV and drove off.

〜

In eight hours flat, he stopped a mile away from the R&D centre at Sonapani. He got off, silently trudging the rest of the way on foot. In twenty minutes, he approached the cave on the ledge. He strode in; darkness was not an issue for him as he crossed the tunnel. The door at the end of the tunnel was solid steel. As he reached it, a laser beam shot out and read his eyes.

The steel door opened silently. Ardhendu walked in.

The underground lab was fabricated of steel. It was soundproof. Operating racks stood in all corners. All sorts of medical testing equipment stood around the hall. Dim lights on the ceiling provided whatever little light the vampires needed.

The thirty-odd beds had thirty men and women strapped to them. They were in a coma. Various tubes were attached to their bodies. Computers monitored their heart rate, metabolism and constantly threw out data on their hemoglobin count and their blood condition. Glucose tubes provided nutrition and proteins directly into their food pipes, while another tube drained de-contaminated blood from them at regular intervals.

At the far end of the hall, two chains hung from the roof. Their ends had large meat hooks attached to them. Two naked male bodies hung from them. Incisions on their feet and neck had tubes which drained their blood into receptacles below.

Ten of RED's remaining scientists worked around them, monitoring their condition. The twenty vampire elite guards were ready to receive Ardhendu. They trained their guns on Ardhendu as the door slammed shut behind him. The guards surrounded him as two of them held his hands back, slipping cuffs on his wrists. They frisked him expertly, removing his jacket and all his weapons, including the test tubes that he had on himself.

When fully secure, they called Colton White in.

"Secure him to that pole. When I am done, he will hang up there." White gestured to the bodies hanging from the meat hooks.

Ardhendu was secured to a pole directly underneath the feet of the two bodies that hung above him.

"Those guys did not respond well to the treatment. So we just killed them. They're meat, you know." White mentioned amiably stabbing the bodies with his thumb.

"Now, let's have a talk, boy…"

"Where is Manoj?"

"Oh, I forgot. A deal is a deal. He's right there." White pointed a remote control to a wall behind him. It slid open from the middle to reveal a dark cell behind a grilled gate. The cell was around a thousand square feet. Around five hundred inmates were dumped in it. Men, women and children in torn and tattered clothes, unwashed, stinking, their feces lining the floor. They huddled around each other screaming in fear, begging to be freed as the wall opened up.

"Manoj Khewsara! Step forward, please!" Colton White yelled. "You have company!"

Manoj emerged from the crowd. He hadn't shaved in days. His clothes were torn. His face was swollen, and he walked with a limp. His eyes were glassy and he hurt all over. On seeing Ardhendu, he ran forward gripping the iron bars of the gate. He screamed in pain as the electric current in them scalded his hands.

"OK, turn it off," White yawned.

Manoj fell to the floor with a crash. He watched Ardhendu from the floor, breathing heavily all the while.

Ardhendu looked straight into the eyes of the only friend he had ever had in this world, of the man who had stood by him when no one else cared; the man who had taken the onus of raising a child who could never even be touched, let alone be raised, by his own biological father.

Ardhendu clenched his teeth till his jaws hurt.

"Look! Like hens in a coup, awaiting turns for their throats to be slit. All of them would make our tables. But that's what the human race is meant to be...our food. You know what a vampire says, when he comes to dinner at a human home?... 'Who's for dinner?' "

White laughed out loud. "What? You don't find this funny? Come on, man! Laugh with me. Come!" The vampires laughed.

Ardhendu watched impassively.

"Man, you need a sense of humour!" White wiped tears from his eyes as he continued to giggle. Then suddenly he smote Ardhendu's jaw. Ardhendu spit blood from his mouth. White paused for a bit. "Hey buddy, I was just warming up man! The best is yet to come."

White brought his left leg up and he kicked Ardhendu straight in the chest. He swung his right hand across Ardhendu's face. Hundreds of stars exploded in Ardhendu's head. He continued to take the punishment until the dullness of the pain began to make the room swim in front of him. Slowly, he began to lose consciousness. White stopped suddenly as he saw Ardhendu's pupils dilate. "Oh whoa! Wait, wait, wait, wait... I'm sorry man, oh no, don't go to sleep on me...we've only just begun...!" he hummed. "Guards!"

They threw buckets of ice-cold water on him.

When Ardhendu came to, White held a syringe in his hand. "Anabolic steroids, right? That's what gives you your added strength, eh? Guess what? I'm gonna give you some. You know why? Because I want you to be conscious as I tear you apart!" White shoved the syringe into Ardhendu's neck.

It wasn't the shot of steroids that woke him up, but the sound of chainsaw...making a trail...on his chest.

"Hold on, son! I'm an artist. I'm trying to make my Mona Lisa here. Ummm, wait a minnit...aah! There she is... The ultimate expression..."

A bloody X stood on Ardhendu's chest. Pain shot through every pore of his body.

"Now, for the coup de grâce! I'm gonna take your leg, your loveliness! What was that dialogue in that Curry Western...oh yeah! Give me your leg, Gabbar...!"

He brought the chainsaw down to Ardhendu's thigh.

Manoj screamed.

White turned around, surprised, "What? You sure you guys aren't gay?"

⌒

The explosion took the wall on the left. The chainsaw flew from White's hands as he fell on the floor. The two vampires standing next to the wall blew up with it.

"Mind if I drop in?" Damon Broadus was at his charming best as he let out a volley of shots from his sub-machine gun. He was dressed in CIA fatigues, zipped from head to toe in combat apparel. It was thick leather over Kevlar. He wore a helmet with a visor on top. Every inch of his body was protected by the material. He caught three of the vampires, the silver bullets searing through them like bolts of lightning. The rest of the vampires ran for cover.

Broadus ran too, towards Ardhendu. He shot through his cuffs at the back, releasing his arms and legs. Ardhendu dropped to his knees.

"You're bleeding! You need first aid!"

"I'll live." Ardhendu panted. "Get the prisoners out first!"

Broadus paused.

Ardhendu looked up at him.

"I don't know what made you come here after me…but I have just one thing to say…"

Broadus smiled, "No man, it's OK…"

"You're a lousy shot. Save your bullets."

Ardhendu got up with a massive effort as the blood oozed from his chest. He stumbled to where his jacket lay. Picking it up, he put it on. He zipped it, then pulled out his semi-automatic. He did not miss, not a single shot. Five vampires lay thrashing on the ground. He ran to the left end of the wall, and punched hard into it. A board with switches appeared behind the broken plaster. He plugged off all the switches.

"Have switched off the electricity! Hurry! Get the prisoners out! Now!"

Broadus ran to the steel bars. He pulled out a can, spraying something which looked like rusty whipped cream on the handle. Then he yelled, "Stand back, all of you!"

The handle shattered into pieces with the explosion.

The inmates rushed out. It was Manoj who shouted at them. "Wait, come with me. We need to get these patients out first! Let's get the stretchers!"

Around ten men stopped. They nodded in unison. Along with Manoj, they began to pick up stretchers. Manoj ran around the people who were in a coma, pulling out needles from their bodies. Within five minutes, the team had them in the stretchers.

"Towards the wall!" Broadus yelled, pointing towards the breach that his first explosion had created. The human mass began to surge forward. *The Red Sea had parted.*

The first burst of flames stopped them in their tracks. Four vampires stood at the breach, big flame throwers in their hands. They were lighting up the walls.

"What the hell are they doing?"

"Setting the R&D lab on fire. They plan to burn all of this and the people down. They can always say, I did it...you know, removing evidence." Ardhendu was faint with pain.

Broadus reached inside his suit. He brought out a spray and without warning, sprayed Ardhendu on his X shaped wound. Ardhendu grimaced in pain.

"It's a clotting agent. It'll hold your wound for twenty-four hours. You'll still need stitches after that."

⁓

The men, women and children screamed in unison. Three of them had been torched.

Ardhendu rushed forward.

"No." Broadus said. "My combat suit is a hi-tech one. Amongst other things, it is also flame resistant. I'll take care of this. You take the people out from the underground escape tunnel!" Broadus pulled his visor down. He added a magazine to his sub-machine gun, then surged ahead.

"Manoj, turn them around! This way!" Ardhendu shouted out. Manoj did so. Ardhendu began to lead them towards the escape hatch.

Broadus approached the vampires.

"Get him!" They yelled. They shot flames at him.

He, in turn, shot them waist downwards.

They watched him as he walked through the fire unscalded as they dropped to the ground. They turned their flame throwers to the ceiling, even as he shot them down, one by one.

The lab was now in flames. Ardhendu used his strength to fling things out of the way as he led the surging mass to the door which was, understandably, locked. He grabbed the two massive handles of the two doors where they met. Using all his strength, he began to pull them apart with hands. They came apart a couple of inches, then slammed shut. He continued like this for ten minutes. But by now most of his strength was gone. He had bled considerably and his limbs gave up. He sat on the floor staring grimly at the fire that spread through the lab. Women covered their children with their bodies. The fire caught one of them. She burnt to death along with her child, whom she had been trying to shield.

Ardhendu watched despondently as his strength ebbed away from him.

It was Manoj who spoke. "We have to work as a team. A lone man cannot do this; we will have to do it together. Half of you on this side, the other half, here. Quick, grab the handles." The handles were long. Long enough for at least ten pairs of hands to grab them from each end. Manoj made the others pull the ones who grabbed the handles. Two teams were formed on both sides, they began to pull…

Broadus fought the vampires fiercely. He had activated the electricity in his suit; any vampire that touched him received a jolt of around 250 volts. He used that stun moment to gun them down. Then he heard the roar.

Turning around, he saw the escape hatch door open just enough to let four or five people out. Manoj was busy directing the women and children to go first. They slipped through quickly while the men held the two doors apart.

Broadus ran towards the door.

Only twenty were left holding the door apart. Ardhendu got up. He lodged himself between the doors, motioning for the others to leave. The men bolted, crawling underneath his legs. Manoj slipped through and so did Damon.

"C'mon man, let go now! Let's go before this place blows up."

Ardhendu looked him in the eye as he strained to keep the gates from shutting.

"I have something to finish." He let go of the gates and they slammed together shutting out Damon and Manoj.

19

Eight inches of snow covered the cottages of Sonapani. The hilltop was a shiny white amongst the red cottages in the pale moonlight. Colton White, who had now gathered the last containers of blood from the main cottage, headed towards the black Scorpio parked along the rough road recently hewed to allow passage to the lab.

It was only when he was ten feet from the SUV that he spied the figure in black standing motionless, almost blending into the black of the vehicle.

White set the containers down to take a better look. The figure stood motionless staring at him.

White shook his head in disbelief. "What, you nuts? I mean, come on now! What are you going to do? Try and stop me from leaving? You're hurt and you've bled. Do you really believe you could defeat me in battle?" White began to reach slowly for the pistol inside his jacket.

"I wouldn't do that. Not right now," Ardhendu said, revealing his semi-automatic.

White smiled. "So that's it, eh? You're now gonna shoot me and be the hero, eh? Typical. Well, what are you waiting for then? Go ahead, finish it."

Ardhendu made no move.

"Well?"

"I am not going to shoot you, White."

"Why?"

"That's too easy."

White shook his head. "You know what, Ardhendu? I always liked you. In you I saw some part of what the human race should have really been. Sincere, hard working, simple dreams…you get the drift? I had really hoped that you would get the picture. But no, you let fear get the better of you. But then that's what humans stand for…fear, of the unknown. Fear, and xenophobia, this world's biggest afflictions. What's been the outcome? War, starvation, destruction, erosion? That's why I detest humans. I mean come on, who wants their food to talk back?"

"Or fight back?" Ardhendu offered dryly.

White glared at him. When he spoke, he did so grimly. "The natural order of things…you've heard of that, haven't you? There's some of the human still left in you. Perhaps, that's one of the reasons why you chose to ensure that they escaped first. But you know what? There's no point in doing so anymore."

Ardhendu did not respond. Nor did he avert his gaze.

"Look at what these humans have done to this world. Climate change, war in the Middle East, terrorism, starvation in Africa, bad loans in the US, forcing thousands out of their homes overnight, water depletion, ozone layer screw-ups, nuclear stockpile build-ups, chemical warfare, mutated strains, bird flu, swine flu…the list is endless. Humans have proliferated on earth, polluting, ruining, eradicating, destroying.

"Five species of animal life disappear every day because humans have released enough carbon gases to make this world uninhabitable for them. All this, and more, has gone on unabated for centuries…and do you know why?"

Ardhendu listened patiently.

"Because humans have no natural predators!"

White paused for a while, then continued. "That's why nature created us. The only species whose natural prey are humans. We are the pure, unadulterated race. We are created for a purpose, to stop human proliferation, to bring order into this world, to claim it as our own. We have been created to bring the human race down and turn them into what they really should be… poultry! So, my friend, now that you see the light, why don't you give up this fight and join us? Think about it, together, we can rule this world."

"White, the only reason I am here is to kill you. So if you're done with your Oscar-night speech, let's get down to business."

White stared at Ardhendu; slowly his blood began to boil. Then he smiled, a cruel predatory smile, his sharp molars reflecting the moonlight. "Alright, but if you really think you're for it, let's do it the way we did it when I was a young man, you know, two hundred years ago? In Transylvania? Man-to-man, hand-to-hand? You game or you gonna chicken out and use that gun on me?"

White took off his jacket and shirt under Ardhendu's watchful eyes. He took off his Rolex and laid the heap carefully on the snow. The muscles of his chest and biceps gleamed in the moonlight. "See? No armaments, we use fists, feet and teeth. How's that?"

Ardhendu dropped his jacket to the ground, took off his T-shirt and turned towards White.

"So it's a fight to the finish, right? No quarter given? No…"

"You talk too much White, I haven't got all night…"

White grinned. "OK. Let's do it."

They hurtled towards each other for the final dance of destruction. The snow flew from underneath their boots as their feet twinkled. The impact knocked both of them away from each other. Ardhendu was thrown back a few feet, and landed heavily on his back; White fell back on the snow, surprised at the strength of his opponent. Both lay still for a while, their bodies shocked by the savage impact.

Ardhendu hurt all over. His strength was slowly ebbing. He felt his wound on his chest. Luckily, the clotting agent held. He forced himself back on his feet. White too was up by now. Dazed by the impact, his rage got the better of him. With a roar he charged at Ardhendu. The two bodies locked on to each other, as they grimaced, each eating into the other's strength, trying to force the other into submission.

Slowly, White moved forward. Then in quick motion, he opened his mouth wide. Sharp fangs dug into both sides of Ardhendu's throat. He struggled, but White's jaws were strong. He held him like a lion holding its prey, sucking the life out of him, slowly, tearing his windpipe. Ardhendu tried to free his hands, but White had them in steely grip. It was impossible to cut loose.

Letting his hands go limp, Ardhendu lifted his right leg, bringing his knee up to White's stomach and kicked him hard. White's jaws did not loosen, but his hands did. Ardhendu used that to shake his hands free. He reached up, forcing his fingers into White's mouth, using all of his strength to pry open White's jaws. Slowly, he managed to pull the sharp teeth away from his now bleeding neck.

White kneeled on the ground, doing his best to loosen Ardhendu's grip, but he held on, straining every muscle to tear the vampire's jaws apart.

White struggled. He dug his nails into Ardhendu's wrists, but Ardhendu did not let go. He then began to pummel Ardhendu with his fists targeting his chest. He still did not let go. Summoning all his strength, he pushed Ardhendu hard, forcing him off the ground. His grip loosened for an instant. White managed to free himself and broke into a run. His jaws hurt badly.

Ardhendu sprang up instantly, landing neatly on White's back. He opened his mouth to reveal his fangs and brought them down on White's neck, holding him in a deathly embrace. White's eyes opened wide with shock and pain. He tried to grab Ardhendu's neck, but failed. White roared. Drops of his blood began to flow down on the snow below. White got up, Ardhendu held on with his teeth, his arms around White's shoulders in a beastly embrace. White shook himself, but Ardhendu did not let go. White screamed in agony. Ardhendu's fangs dug deeper. He began to push Ardhendu back with his weight, banging him repeatedly against the trunk of a tree. Ardhendu shook like a leaf, hanging on at times only with his fangs. White continued the onslaught.

Finally when his back could not take the tree any more, Ardhendu let go, falling to the ground. He felt the world swirl around him.

Holding his bleeding neck, White shuffled towards the SUV. He opened the hatch and pulled out a long sword. Ardhendu got up with some effort, ran to his fallen jacket, and pulled out the switchblades.

White advanced. He swung his sword at Ardhendu, who captured it smoothly between the switchblades. White went once again for Ardhendu who held the sword with his blades trying to stop it from slashing his throat. Then suddenly, Ardhendu swung around with his switchblades aiming for White's neck. White stepped back just as quickly, as the switchblades whizzed past. Lifting his sword, he swung it hard. It took one switchblade and slashed it into half.

Ardhendu rushed towards the watch tower with just one switchblade in hand, with White in pursuit. Ardhendu ran up the spiral staircase to the first floor. The sword had taken a piece of his jacket, but the Kevlar had protected him from too much damage. White followed, a murderous rage burning in his eyes.

Ardhendu stopped at the landing on the first floor swinging his blade at White. He was no match for the bigger man with the sword. Ardhendu ran up the stairs to the second floor landing. White bounded up the stairs after him. Ardhendu jumped, the sword narrowly missing his torso, then bounded up the next two flights of stairs, panting heavily. He had reached the top floor of the watch tower. It was a small ten by ten feet room, made completely of wood, with two-way windows covered with dark film. It was a matter of seconds before White caught up with Ardhendu.

The two predators faced each other like gladiators in a packed arena. White thrust out his sword, Ardhendu parried with his switchblade. The sword caught the back of his hand, leaving a bloody gash. The switchblade fell to the floor. Without stopping, White swung his sword again, tearing open the wound on Ardhendu's chest. Ardhendu grunted. The wound opened up, making way for the blood. He was still for a second, and then he fell hard on the wooden floor. He lay there, defeated. Then he looked up helplessly as White lifted the sword with both his hands.

"I am Colton White, fourth in line from Prince Vlad. Prince of the vampires, ruler of humans. You really thought you could defeat me?" He bent over Ardhendu, raising his sword high above his head aiming for the fallen man's head. The fight had now gone out of Ardhendu. A plea for deliverance was all that remained in his now dimming eyes.

White saw that very clearly. Suddenly, he stopped. He stared at Ardhendu, his heart filling up with an unexplained empathy for the fallen one. After all, Ardhendu had put up a good fight; firm and fair. Just like the old days. White couldn't bring himself to slay him anymore. So he lowered the sword.

"I can't kill you Ardhendu, it's not fair, you are after all, unarmed. I have been unfair in this fight. Let's stop this. You go your way and I'll go mine. Let our paths never cross each other. We've both been right in our own ways and perhaps we've both been wrong too. We'll achieve nothing by killing each other. I shall disappear from this world and so shall RED. Let's end it here," he reasoned as he flung his sword away.

That was when Ardhendu brought his knees up to his own chest, while pushing his elbows on to the floor, and shot both his feet up, kicking White squarely on the chest. Caught unaware, White hit the wooden ceiling of the watch tower. The wood splintered easily as White's body shot out of the ceiling. The air outside was cold.

At that precise moment, a giant red ball began to rise in the sky. Its rays pierced through the dark sky, turning the snowy white peaks into a fiery red! Caught mid-air, White turned his head towards that ball and screamed.

His eyes caught fire. His tongue which protruded from his mouth burnt next. His body began a forty feet descent to the ground as the rising sun burnt his head, throat, chest and torso. His legs caught fire as he hit the ground hard. The sun consumed him mercilessly. He twitched violently and then, like a gunshot, his skull exploded.

Ardhendu stood at the window of the watch tower looking down at the uneven patch of ash on the snow. His lips moved soundlessly, "Goodbye, Prince! Shouldn't have taken off your designer watch."

20

Damon finished bandaging Ardhendu's wounds carefully avoiding contact with his blood. "There, that should hold you for a while."

Manoj approached, trudging through the snow. They sat at the porch of the dining hall of Sonapani.

"Thanks, man…"

Ardhendu gestured to him to stop. "Go back and look after your wife and the child. Take care of them…and… Don't let my son ever know that his father is a monster."

"You're not a monster," Manoj said quietly.

Ardhendu stared at his friend, then turned his face to the sun.

❧

"Where would you go now?" Broadus asked.

"I haven't thought about it yet."

"Well, the Nepal border isn't far away, I could smuggle you there and get you to the Philippines into one of the CIA bases. My superiors are OK with the idea of taking up the research where your father left off; we could find a way forward for your condition."

"What do I have to do in return?"

"Become a CIA mercenary. Lead the war on behalf of the CIA by weeding out all the vampires in this world. You've wiped out RED in India, but they have arms in other countries. What do you say?"

Ardhendu looked up at Broadus. He had a half-smile on his face. "There's no free lunch, eh?"

"There's no free lunch!" Broadus agreed with a grin.

"We even have a code for you."

"Yeah? What's that?"

"Code RED!"